NEGOTIATING
FOR LOVE

SHARON C. COOPER

Negotiating for Love

By: Sharon C. Cooper

Copyright © 2016 by Sharon C. Cooper

ISBN: 978-0-9903505-9-0
Book Cover: Selestiele Designs
Editor: Yolanda Barber - Write Time, Write Place
Formatted by: Enterprise Book Services, LLC
Published by: Amaris Publishing LLC in the United States

Disclaimer

CHAPTER ONE

"PJ, I'm going to kill you." Martina "MJ" Jenkins jerked out of the chair and snatched up her jacket. She weaved between tables that were too close together, her heart pounding like a fat man on a treadmill, chasing a cheeseburger. She couldn't get to the exit fast enough. The door came into view, and she stormed out of the hotel's banquet room with her cousin, Peyton, hot on her heels.

"Will you slow down?" Peyton Jenkins whispered through gritted teeth. "God, you are so childish. I knew it was a mistake to have you come with me. I can't believe you acted a complete fool in there."

Martina came to an abrupt stop and spun on her three-inch heels. Heels she hated wearing. Heels she was about ready to rip off and throw at someone. Peyton to be exact.

Peyton knew better than anyone that Martina would much rather be in a T-shirt and jeans, her usual attire. Instead, she had dressed in a silk blouse, black pencil skirt, and stupid nylons. Who the heck wore nylons these days anyway?

She faced her cousin, careful to keep a little distance for fear of popping Peyton.

"I can't believe you did this to me. You set me up!" Martina stabbed a finger in the air. "You knew *he* was going to be here and didn't tell me. How could you?"

Peyton planted her hands on her hips. "How could I what? Not tell you that *Senator Paul Kendricks*, who you don't even know but despise, was the guest speaker at the breakfast today?"

"Exactly. You know how I feel about that … that egotistical jerk. You could have come by yourself or heck, brought someone else."

The day before, Peyton suggested they attend the breakfast since they both oversaw the operations of Jenkins & Sons Construction, the family business their grandfather, Steven Jenkins, started years ago. Upon his retirement, Peyton, an electrician by trade, took on the enormous responsibility of becoming the senior manager and Martina was second in command.

Peyton gripped Martina's arm and pulled her further away from the doors of the banquet room. "Have you totally lost your mind? When Grampa finds out what you did, he is going to wring your bony little neck. I have never been so embarrassed in all of my life."

"Then you shouldn't have insisted that I come!" Martina pointed toward the room. "You had to know that I would tell him what I think about his policies."

"You didn't just tell him what you thought, MJ. You called the poor guy every frickin' name except his own. That man is a U.S. Senator. You didn't have to embarrass me *and* disrespect him in front of all of those people."

Martina said nothing. Maybe she had overreacted. She couldn't help herself. Not only had she been shocked to see him, but the fact that he was still talking crazy bugged the heck out of her. An advocate for trade unions, she hated that the governor and his minions were working overtime to weaken labor organizations. In some cases, it was with the help of unions that people who looked like her, black and a woman, even had a chance to get into the construction trades.

"I am so tired of him and his cohorts. He has to know how much the changes he's promoting will hurt the working class. Actually, he probably knows. He just doesn't care!"

"Stop it!" After glancing around to see if anyone could hear them Peyton stood in front of Martina. "You know what, MJ? I get that you're mad about what the governor is trying to do and in some aspects, I agree with you. What I don't agree with is how you made a complete fool of yourself in there and showed your tail. Something else I don't understand. There are plenty of politicians pushing for the same changes that Senator Kendricks is promoting. Yet, your anger is directed at him and not the others. Why is that?"

"I've had enough. I'm out of here." Martina marched down the multi-color carpeted hallway in search of the nearest exit.

She took about ten steps before Peyton called out.

"The breakfast is not over. Besides, how are you planning to get home? Did you forget that I drove?"

Oh, crap. Martina stopped and huffed. With her hands on her hips, she gave a cursory glance around willing herself to calm down. A sitting area with a sofa and two leather chairs looked inviting, but she wouldn't be able to sit still. What she needed was some fresh air.

She finally turned. Peyton stood in the middle of the hallway, arms folded across her chest and foot tapping like some warden, impatiently waiting.

Martina wasn't going back into that room. She meant everything she said and going back in wouldn't be a good idea. There was no telling what else would fly out of her mouth. She wasn't known for having tact. According to her cousins and everyone else who knew her, she didn't have a filter and was quick to say whatever popped into her mind.

"I'll wait out here if you're planning to stay until the end."

"Fine."

Martina moved toward a pair of chairs and a small round table less than five feet away. She hated attending events where she had to get dressed up and sit quietly through a program. And when one of the speakers happened to be an enemy, it was like having to endure a root canal.

"Martina!"

She froze. Her breath lodged in her throat and hands fisted at her sides. That deep, baritone voice had always had an effect on her, even when she didn't want it to and today was no different. Her pulse pounded an erratic cadence in her ears as a war raged within her on whether or not to turn around.

"You were brazen enough to spout out that nonsense in there, yet you're not brave enough to look at me."

The annoyance that consumed her only moments ago returned and she spun in the direction of the voice. But the smart retort dangling on the end of her tongue, dropped off. Instead, all she could do was stand cemented in place and stare at the man who stirred so many emotions within her.

Senator Paul Kendricks. Part of her wanted to pick up the small table near her leg and fling it at him. Whereas the other part of her was taken back to every one of her erotic dreams he had starred in.

She wanted to hate him. God, she wanted to hate him. She couldn't. For reasons she didn't want to revisit at the moment, she knew she would never hate him.

Martina took in his appearance, assessing his smooth dark skin, intense brown eyes, and those luscious lips that were tempting whether smiling or tilted down in a frown the way they were now.

Fury and sexual tension battled within her. On one hand, she wanted to wrap her hands around his thick neck and shake him. But on the other hand, she wanted to fall into him, feel his powerful arms wrapped around her while she tasted his sweet lips. She knew they were delicious because she'd tasted them before, on more than one occasion in fact.

Her gaze took in his perfectly groomed mustache. Normally he was clean-shaven, a preference for those in the Senate, but not a requirement. Though not today. Today the light sprinkle of scruff shadowing his cheek and chin, made him look even sexier than usual.

His broad shoulders and fit body were sheathed in a tailored suit that she knew cost more than she made in a week, made her remember. Made her remember how good-looking he was. Made her remember how being anywhere near him sent tingles through her body. And made her remember why seeing Paul up close and personal again wasn't a good idea.

"Hi Senator Kendricks, I'm Peyton Jenkins. I'm so sorry for my cousin's behavior. I assure you, she will not be returning to the event. She tends to speak before thinking sometimes and—"

"I'm well aware of Martina's penchant for speaking her mind, even at the most inopportune times," Paul said, his gaze never leaving Martina. "It's good to see you again, Martina."

The way her name slid out of his mouth sent a sweet thrill up her spine, licking her skin like a gentle breeze. She loathed that his voice still had the power to stop her in her tracks. What she hated, even more, was the desire radiating in his eyes. The same desire was coursing through her veins.

Ughhh, she growled silently, pissed that she was still attracted to the man.

"Too bad I can't say the same about you." Her throat tightened at the words that opposed what she truly felt inside. Her voice no longer carried the same annoyance from earlier. Instead, she sounded more breathy than she intended.

Damn him for looking so good.

"Hold up. Wait." Peyton stood with her mouth hanging open, her gaze bouncing between them. "You two know each other?"

"As a matter of fact we do," Paul volunteered. "Your cousin and I know each other *very* well."

"Really, MJ?"

Martina's shoulders slumped and she groaned, knowing she was going to get an ear full on the way home. How many times had she talked nonsense to Peyton about hating this man?

"Tell her, Martina."

"Stop calling me that!" she fumed.

"That's your name. What else would you have me call you?" Paul folded his thick arms across his chest making his six foot, two-hundred-pound stature appear even more imposing.

Martina risked moving closer with every intention of telling him off but pulled up short. His intoxicating scent wrapped around her, weakening her resolve. An invisible force pushed her to step forward, but she fought to maintain control. If she were any closer to him, she might do something stupid like leap into his arms and devour his mouth.

She sucked in a deep breath and released it slowly while straightening her shoulders.

"I would prefer you not call me anything. As far as I'm concerned, you can forget my name and everything about me."

Silence. Instead of responding, his gaze traveled slowly down her body from the top of her curly hair and didn't stop until he reached her black pumps. He repeated the gesture in reverse, but this time his gaze lingered on her breasts. Her nipples hardened against her satin bra as he visually caressed her.

Martina swallowed hard under his perusal, cursing her body for desiring more than just his visual attention.

His eyes met hers once again. "That will never happen, Martina. I will never forget anything about you."

CHAPTER TWO

Paul couldn't stop staring. He originally came into the hallway with every intention of giving Martina a piece of his mind. Yet, all he wanted to do was pull her into his arms, feel the softness of her body against his and taste those sweet, familiar lips. But he knew better. He knew this woman well enough to know that she would probably slug him in the chest if he even tried.

His gaze raked over her body a third time. So different, yet so familiar. Her long straight hair was now curly and much shorter, stopping at her shoulders. He used to run his fingers through those tresses, appreciating the softness of each strand. Though he loved the old style, he had to admit that even this new look, curls with blond highlights, was just as beautiful.

Hell, who was he kidding? Everything about the woman was gorgeous from her blemish-free, cafe au lait skin to her slim, but curvaceous figure. Considering they dated for six months, he couldn't ever remember her in a skirt. And seeing those long legs of hers that had been wrapped around his waist more times than he could count, sent blood rushing to a certain part of his anatomy.

His pulse quickened. He forced himself to stay planted in that spot despite the way her scent – a combination of soap and baby powder – teased his senses making him want to reach for her.

Damn this woman for still having an effect on him.

Seeing her in the fitted blouse and the almost too short skirt brought back memories of hot, unabashed lovemaking. The phrase *live out loud* fit Martina Jenkins perfectly. She didn't do anything half way, whether it was building a porch or bringing him to his knees in the heat of passion. She was the most amazing woman he had ever known inside and outside of the bedroom.

God, he missed her.

"I see you're still talking that trash about how snatching the union's bargaining rights is going to be best for the state of Ohio in the long run," Martina seethed.

And there went the fantasy.

"Why would you come to an event where I'm speaking, if you're so against everything I say?" Realizing his voice had grown louder with each word, he lowered it. "Why are you here, Martina, if you hate me so much?"

Noticing that she, at least, had the decency to look contrite made him recognize how much emotion he'd put into his last words. He couldn't help it. They were once so good together and then all of sudden, poof, their relationship was over.

She stepped back and turned slightly away from him, running her fingers through her mass of curls. He groaned when her blouse lifted slightly revealing taut, smooth skin that he yearned to touch.

"I don't hate you," she said quietly and dropped her shoulders. "I just hate everything you stand for."

Well, that was progress since she had called him Satan's spawn minutes ago, in a room full of spectators.

He had spotted her earlier when she strolled into the banquet room before sitting at a table in the middle of the space. At first, he thought his eyes were playing tricks on him, knowing she would never show up at an event where he was the keynote speaker. Once she had settled in her seat, it was as if she felt his attention on her. She did a slow turn and their gazes met. Her eyes grew large, and mouth dropped open, but she quickly recovered. Shock immediately turned into disgust or maybe anger. He wasn't quite sure.

Studying Martina now, everything he had once felt for her came rushing back. Admiration. Attraction. Love. Despite her inability to think before she spoke, she was one of the sweetest people he had ever known and the only woman he had fallen in love with.

"Can we go somewhere and talk?" he asked.

This wasn't what he originally planned to say, yet, he wanted to be in her presence just a little longer. There were a number of questions that plagued his mind since the last time he'd seen her a year ago. He needed answers. Suddenly it didn't matter that she had called him everything but a child of God only minutes ago.

"Hell no, you can't talk to me! As long as you're talkin' crazy about the state stripping unions of their bargaining rights, you and I have nothing to say to each other." She turned and stormed away.

"Martina!" Paul started after her but stopped when she picked up speed. Running away from him apparently wasn't enough. She lifted her hand and gave him the finger without missing a step.

Infuriating, loud-mouth, stubborn woman.

He watched her and Peyton exit the building through a side door. She was the most pigheaded woman he had ever known. Why'd he even bother trying to talk to her? It was useless trying to get her to do anything she didn't want to do.

Paul didn't know how long he stood there before feeling a presence behind him and then there was laughter. Not a chuckle, but an outright, deep belly laugh. He didn't have to turn to know who it belonged to. Davion, his cousin, who happened to be his best friend, grinned like an idiot as he approached.

"Did that woman just tell you to get lost and then give you the finger?" Davion could barely get the words out before he fell out laughing all over again.

Paul didn't bother responding. The whole morning had been one verbal battle after another. First with his matchmaking mother, and then his father who was living vicariously through Paul's political career, and now Martina.

"So that's her, huh?" Davion asked. He dabbed at his eyes with the heel of his hands, a grin still covering his mouth.

Paul frowned when he thought about Davion's question. "Her who?"

"The woman who has had you all twisted up inside

for the past year. I caught a little of the conversation."

Paul scrubbed his hands down his face. He never told anyone about Martina, not because he hadn't wanted to. Definitely not because he hadn't wanted to. Each time he asked her to be his date for an event or invited her to his parent's home for dinner, she had always turned him down. As far as she was concerned, they weren't dating, they'd been *hanging out*. Her words, not his. Somehow in the six months that they had dated, he fell in love.

Hell, he loved everything about the woman from her wit to her fearlessness. He even loved that she said whatever was on her mind. Add her love of sports, food, and their incredible sex life to the equation, and he'd been a goner within weeks of meeting her.

It wasn't until he had spoken those three little words, I love you, did she start changing. Slowly she pulled away from him, canceling their dates, and finding every excuse not to see him.

"No need trying to deny it," Davion said. So caught up in his thoughts, Paul had forgotten Davion was standing there. "The answer is written all over your face. But what I don't understand, is why you never mentioned that little spitfire."

He'd never mentioned her because she treated him like some dirty little secret. Though he had been able to talk her into going out sometimes to bistros, the movies and a few sporting events, she preferred they stayed behind closed doors.

Their last argument invaded his mind. Frustration stirred inside his gut the way it had back then. Martina walked out on him claiming it was because of his political platform, but he knew her departure was about something more. Unfortunately, he never bothered to find out what. He'd had enough. The disagreements and secrecy had taken its toll by then.

"So are you going to continue standing there looking goofy, or are you going to tell me about her? Who is she? Seeing how passionately she cursed you out in there, I assume she knows someone in a union."

Paul hadn't seen Martina in a year. He had finally come to grips with losing her and had moved on. But now, after seeing her again, he wasn't so sure it was possible to move on from Martina Jenkins.

"She's a carpenter."

Davion's eyebrows shot up. "Get the heck out of here. Seriously?"

Paul nodded, an involuntary smile spreading across his lips. He would never forget the first day he'd met her. He didn't know what captured his attention first, her lovely face, that shapely ass encased in the tightest jeans he'd seen on a woman, or the construction boots. Then she opened her mouth and started talking sports to the other construction workers who she'd been with. Paul had fallen for her at that moment. But it had taken him three attempts before she finally agreed to give him her telephone number.

"Carpenters definitely look different these days." Davion shoved his hands into the front pockets of his pants. "So I assume there's a history between you two. What happened?"

Paul didn't want to discuss Martina. Heck, he was still trying to come to grips that he had seen her again. It had been a long time. Too long.

"We didn't work out." He glanced at his watch and nodded toward the banquet room. "I should probably get back in there." He stepped around Davion, but his cousin blocked his path.

"Not before I hear about the firecracker who made steam come out your ears. Spill it. You can even give me the CliffsNotes version."

Paul sighed and ran his hand over his low cut hair.

"I met her at a coffee shop, and we hung out for a few months."

"So what went wrong?"

Paul shrugged. "I'm not sure, man. We never really talked about what went wrong. One thing I do know is that we wanted different things. I wanted marriage and a family, and she wanted a sex partner. I was tired of being her dirty little secret, boy-toy, or whatever you want to call it. She moved on, and so did I."

Paul knew early in their relationship that Martina didn't want the same things out of life when it came to marriage and children, but he hadn't wanted to lose her. He stopped bringing up marriage as a topic for discussion.

Paul lifted his head to find Davion standing with his arms folded and eyes narrowed.

"What?"

"Hanging out in D.C. with all of those stuffed shirts must have finally gotten to you. That's the only explanation I can come up with that can explain how my woman-magnet cousin let a fine piece of tail like the carpenter go. And she wasn't hounding you for a commitment. Really?" Davion shook his head. "Let me get my hands on a hottie like that—"

"And I will knock you the hell out," Paul growled and jerked hard on his cousin's lapels.

They hadn't fought since they were kids when they both fell for Jasmine Conner. Sure Martina looked like every man's fantasy woman, but he would not stand there and listen to Davion or any other man talk about all he wanted to do to her.

"I'm not playin' D. Every one of your perfectly straight teeth will be lying on the ground if I find out you stepped to her."

Davion shrugged out of Paul's grasp. "Man, I don't want your leftovers. I don't care how fine she might be. You know me better than that. I might talk trash, but I have *never* done any shit like step to someone you've dated!"

Paul glanced around, hoping no one had witnessed his momentary lapse. He dropped his head and rubbed the back of his neck.

"You're right. I'm trippin'. Sorry about that."

"Your ass is more than trippin'. I don't know exactly all that transpired between you two, but clearly you haven't moved on the way you claim."

Paul didn't want to admit it, but he knew Davion was right. There were plenty of days that he had thought about Martina and didn't act on the desire to contact her. Yet today, after seeing those fiery brown eyes and pouty lips, need churned within him. He needed to talk to her. He needed to know why she had walked out on him, and he was finally ready to hear her reason. Unlike before, when he hadn't cared to take the time to know.

Davion rubbed his chin. "Well, I'll be damn. It's worse than I thought."

Paul waved him off and dropped into the nearest chair. There was no sense going back into the banquet room at this point. His reappearance would only distract the current speaker. But he wasn't sure he wanted to sit in the hallway either, especially with

Davion wearing that stupid grin.

"It's no wonder you haven't wanted to hang out as much when you're in town." Davion sat on the arm of a chair across from Paul. "I knew it probably had something to do with a woman, but I didn't know it was like this."

Paul didn't bother asking what he meant by "like this." He was sure he didn't want to know.

"How long are you going to pine over this spitfire?"

"Martina. Her name is Martina." Paul smiled at how angry she'd gotten when he called her Martina. She preferred MJ, but he had refused to use her nickname. He had once told her that Martina was a beautiful name for a very beautiful woman.

Knowing that his cousin was still waiting for a response, Paul leaned forward in his seat, his elbows on his thighs.

"Man, it's been a year. I'm not pining over her. I've moved on."

Davion shook his head and chuckled. "You definitely haven't moved on."

"You don't know what you're talking about."

"I do, but since you think you've moved on, we can double date tonight. My girl has a friend, and she's been trying to get me to fix the two of you up."

"Not interested."

"Trust me man, when you get a look at Peppermint, you're going to be thanking me."

Paul's mouth twitched. "Peppermint? Her name is Peppermint."

"Yeah, but don't judge the woman by her name," Davion said with a straight face.

"Is she a stripper or something? I have a

reputation to protect. The last thing I need is a scandal centered on someone named *Peppermint*." He shook his head. "No way has her parents named her Peppermint."

"Man, her name is beside the point. When you see her, her name is going to be the last thing on your mind. She's a little quiet, unlike *Martina*, but I think you'll like her. So are you in? Or are you going to admit that you're still hung up on that hot tamale who just left?"

Paul couldn't believe he was seriously considering going out with someone named after a hard piece of candy. Yet, this might be a way for him to prove not only to Davion that he'd moved on, but also to himself.

"Set it up, but I better not regret this."

CHAPTER THREE

Martina couldn't get to Peyton's car fast enough. The jackhammer pounding inside her chest had her breaths coming hard and fast. She marched between parked cars on wobbly legs trying like crazy to tune out her cousin's constant yammering.

"You and Senator Paul Kendricks had a fling. The moment he said, *I will never forget anything about you,* I knew. That is frickin' unbelievable!" Peyton unlocked the doors to her Chevy Malibu. "When I tell the others, they are going to flip!"

Martina dropped into the car and slammed the door, wishing she could just make herself disappear. She and Paul were able to keep their relationship a secret for six months. Today, after a year of being apart, their secret was out. During the past year, she had badmouthed Paul and his policies to her cousins, threatening to behead them if they so much as mentioned his name in her presence. Now, once Peyton told them the real deal, they were never going to let her live this down.

Martina laid her head against the headrest. Just thinking about Paul made her stomach do somersaults. They didn't travel in the same circles and with him spending much of his time in D.C., she was comfortable in knowing that she probably would never see him face to face again. But now that she had, would she be able to stop thinking about him?

"All this time, you made the Senator look like the enemy." Peyton pulled out of the hotel's parking lot.

"He is the enemy! What he and his cohorts are trying to do is downright cruel."

"Yeah, but you were sleeping with the enemy, MJ!"

"Who said I slept with him? Not once in that brief conversation back there did either of us say that we slept together."

"Ha! Are you kidding me? It's a wonder all three of us didn't go up in flames with the sparks bouncing between you two. I have known you all of your life and *never* have I seen you react to any man that way."

Martina stared out the passenger window, the scenery passing by in a blur. She couldn't deny her cousin's observation. Her whole body had heated with desire the moment Paul called her name, and then she turned around.

She shivered remembering how enticing he looked in his navy blue, pinstriped suit.

"We are having a girl's night at your house tonight. Actually, I don't think this can wait. I need to get the cousins together now. There is no way we're letting you off the hook on this one. Get ready to tell us everything!"

"There's nothing to tell." Martina lied. There was so much she could tell. Like how whenever he kissed her angels sang in the background. Or how there had never been a time when a man's hands had affected her so profoundly. His touch alone made her panties damp, and her toes curl.

Oh yeah, she could tell them stories that would have them fanning themselves.

"Quit playing," Peyton chided. "I'm sure there's a lot to tell. What you need to be concerned about is what Grampa is going to say when he finds out how you represented the company this morning. I've seen you open your big mouth and say some crazy stuff, but today I almost didn't recognize you."

The conversation with their grandfather was one she was not looking forward to. Steven Jenkins was serious about how his children and grandchildren represented the company and the family. He didn't tolerate public displays of ignorance.

You're a reflection of me, and you're a reflection of this family. The choices you make don't only affect you, they affect all of us in some way. He would say in his deep baritone voice.

She'd be ready. It wouldn't be the first time that he had to give her one of his speeches, and she was pretty sure it wouldn't be the last. Besides, if he could get over the time her cousin Toni ended up, unknowingly, at a drug house and got arrested, he could get over anything.

Fifteen minutes later, they pulled up to Martina's small bungalow. She was so tired of hearing Peyton go on and on about how she had bamboozled her and their cousins all this time about Paul. Sure she had called him a louse, who shouldn't be allowed to represent the state. And maybe she had compared him and his senator cohorts to cockroaches, but still.

Her cousins couldn't hold that against her.

Martina had to admit that she might've gone overboard the past year or so regarding her feelings about Paul. In all honesty, he was a good man. As a senator, he had done a lot in proposing and supporting bills that had helped the country as a whole. It hadn't been until the past year, when he supported the governor's idea about taking some of the power from unions, that had her seeing red. She didn't hate him though she wanted to since he had reneged on his agreement to her while they were dating.

"Let's get back to you and the *Senator*."

"Let's not," Martina said as they walked up the stairs to the house.

Peyton's cell phone rang and Martina hoped it was a call that could save her from the interrogation she knew was coming.

Martina unlocked the front door and stepped into the house with Peyton pulling up the rear talking on her cell phone to their cousin Toni. Martina tuned out the conversation, dropped her purse on the sofa, and headed to the small half-bath steps away from the living room.

Washing her hands, she took notice of the new mirror she had recently installed over the pedestal sink. She was on the tail end of finishing the renovations in the home that was her latest flip. Buying and selling houses for the past five years, this was the only one she had moved into while doing the renovations.

Normally the homes she purchased weren't in the best of neighborhoods and some weren't even livable initially. This one had been different. She had fallen in love with not only the neighborhood but also the small bungalow. She was tempted to hold on to the home instead of selling it, but she stood to make almost twice as much money as she'd paid.

Martina walked the short distance to the kitchen. Despite not needing as much work as some of the others, the house had taken her a little longer to complete. Attending night school to finish her bachelor's degree in business, and all the extra hours she'd been putting in at work had slowed progress on the home.

"Girl, I know. I almost fell over when I realized they knew each other." Martina overheard Peyton say.

She rolled her eyes and grabbed two small bottles of orange juice from the refrigerator. Setting the bottles down on the black quartz countertop, she glanced at the local newspaper spread open to an article that featured Paul. Speculation was growing about a possible run for the presidency during the next election.

Martina sipped her juice. Reading the article before leaving home, she wished it would have made mention that Paul would be a guest speaker at the event she and Peyton had just attended. Although, maybe it had mentioned the event. She had only scanned the article. Instead, her attention had locked onto the photo of him. Even now, his handsome face held her attention. His intelligent, sexy eyes drew her in every time, punctuated by his beautiful smile that highlighted those full tempting lips.

A swarm of butterflies fluttered in her gut. She still hadn't recovered from the shock of seeing him in person. Even now, thinking about the man had her body prickling with need. While they were together, he had been an addiction she couldn't shake, and there were still days she suffered through withdrawal.

"Have CJ pick up a pizza on her way," Peyton said of her sister Christina, her voice interrupting Martina's thoughts. "You know we're not going to get any information out of MJ if we don't feed her."

"Don't talk about me like I'm not here," Martina snapped. The kitchen overlooked the living room where Peyton lounged on the leather sofa. "She can bring as much pizza as she wants. I'm still not telling you busybodies anything."

"Oh, I forgot CJ is sick." Peyton ignored Martina as she continued her conversation. She shook out of the jacket that matched her navy blue skirt and tossed it on a nearby chair. "Serves her right for letting MJ goad her into eating that ginormous hamburger last night, knowing she hadn't eaten meat in a year."

A smile lifted the corners of Martina's mouth as she folded the newspaper. It wasn't funny that Christina, the flower child of the family was sick, but then again, it was a little funny. Martina didn't know what her cousin was thinking. Christina had been a vegetarian for the past year and suddenly decided she wanted a burger. Martina might've taunted her some, but she didn't think her cousin would fall off the wagon the way she had.

"MJ, you know you're going to have to give us something." Peyton strolled into the kitchen stuffing her cell phone into the side pocket of her skirt and accepted the bottle of juice Martina offered. "I don't know why you've kept this a secret anyway. And I can't help but wonder how you were able to date him without any of us finding out."

That surprised Martina too. Though the majority

of her and Paul's times together were behind closed doors, they did go out periodically. What they enjoyed most, besides sex, was cooking together. They both were excellent cooks, but Paul was the best. He had once admitted that if he could do anything, he'd open a small bistro in Cincinnati and be a guest chef occasionally.

"So what happened? Why'd you guys stop seeing each other?"

"He was getting too serious, and he wanted to go public."

Peyton's hand stilled. The bottle of juice less than an inch from her lips.

"So let me get this right. You broke things off with the Senator because he wanted to tell people you two were in a relationship?"

Martina sighed dramatically. "PJ, I don't want to talk about this."

Martina left the kitchen and strolled into the living room, hoping to catch a football game. Since she didn't have to work that weekend, she'd planned to attend the breakfast and then spend the rest of the day camped out in front of her television.

"I'm not leaving until I get some details." Peyton sat next to her on the sofa and kicked off her navy blue, pointy-toe pumps. "So give me something."

"You're starting to become as irritating as Toni and Jada." Those two cousins were the gossipers in the family. Always in everyone's business. "What happened between Paul and me is none of your business."

Peyton rolled her eyes and sipped the juice before setting it on one of the football coasters on top of the cocktail table.

"I'm waiting. How long did you two date?"

"We…we didn't really date. We just hung out. Nothing more."

"So for how long?"

Martina glared at her.

"How long, MJ?"

"Six months." Six glorious months. The best months of her life. Paul had treated her like a precious gift. Their times together were like scenes from a romance novel.

"That has to be a record for you. You have never been with any man that long."

"I wasn't *with* him! We were just…we were just hanging out. Nothing serious. But then he had to go and ruin things by trying to turn our relationship into more than it was."

"So you admit that it was a relationship?"

Martina dropped her head against the back of the sofa and groaned. Her cousin was like a pesky mosquito, buzzing around trying to draw blood.

"We were friends, PJ."

"Friends with benefits?"

Martina hesitated, staring up at the new Inca bronze light fixture before finally saying, "Yes."

A flashback of their last time together clouded her mind. Heat rose to her cheeks as a memory of their sweat-slicked bodies, intertwined limbs and breathing so heavy it was as if she could still hear them panting after a round of mind-blowing sex.

Normally after a lovemaking session, they'd either pass out or shower together, but that night had been different. He had been different. His body had hovered above her, his intense eyes stared down into hers, and she knew. She knew that his feelings for her had changed. Hell her feelings had changed too, but she had no intention of ruining what they had by voicing what was swirling around in her heart.

"MJ," Peyton called out several times, waving her hand in front of Martina's face. "MJ!"

Martina sat up straighter. "What?"

A knowing smile spread across her cousin's face. "So Senator Kendricks must have some serious game if he has you zoning out like this. Why'd you guys break up? I mean, why did you two stop *hanging out?*"

"I just told you. The jerk ruined our agreement!" She sat forward and shoved her hands through her hair, mentally shaking off the memory that had invaded her brain. "He started getting too serious. Before we hooked up, we both agreed to keep things light. We were supposed to be just having a little fun and then all of a sudden, bam! He wanted more."

"And that's a bad thing?

"He changed the rules."

"Were you guys exclusive?"

"Well…kinda, but—"

"No buts. You were technically a couple. Why wouldn't he want more? Most normal people would want more."

"Well, I didn't!" Martina shot out of her seat and paced in front of the sofa.

"Like I said, most normal people would want more."

"Whatever." Why was she letting Peyton get inside of her head? She and Paul were over. She didn't have to answer questions or remember. Hell, she didn't want to remember that time in her life.

Paul is my past. I have moved on.

"Oh. My. God. You're in love with him!"

"What?" Martina jammed her hands onto her hips. "What is wrong with you? How the heck did you get that out of anything I just said? I am *not* in love with Paul Kendricks or anyone for that matter."

"Yeah, tell it to someone who didn't see you two together today." Peyton stood, her arms folded across her chest. "When you weren't scowling at him, it was written all over your face. Like it is now. You can lie to me, but you might as well stop lying to yourself. You fell in love with that man."

"You know good and damn well I don't do the whole falling in love crap! *Never* will I allow myself to be subjected to something that only ends in heartbreak."

"I'd bet my next paycheck that you're still in love with Senator Kendricks," Peyton continued as if Martina hadn't said anything. "Does any of this have to do with your mother?"

"Peyton," she said in a threatening tone, willing her not to bring Carolyn Jenkins into the conversation.

"MJ, you are nothing like Aunt Carolyn if that's what you're worried about."

Martina threw up her arms and let them fall to her sides. "I don't have time for this nonsense. I'm done talking to you." She headed for the hall that led to the three bedrooms. "Oh and when the girls get here, don't bother bringing up Paul's name or *my mother* for that matter. I'm done talking!"

I am not my mother, and I'm done thinking about Paul.

CHAPTER FOUR

The next day, Paul sat in the back of the coffee shop in what was once his favorite booth, sipping a cup of black coffee. Leaving home that morning, he had no intention of stopping, but before he knew it, he was pulling into the parking lot of Java Café.

He took another sip of the super-hot coffee, his attention on the entrance. He didn't know why he looked up every time the door chimed. Then again, who was he kidding? He knew why. This was where he and Martina had first met.

He set his cup down and rubbed his eyes. Why was he even there? After he and Martina had broken up, he hadn't stepped foot in the place for fear of running into her. It wasn't hard at first because he had poured himself into his work, even spending time in D.C. whether the Senate was in session or not. Cincinnati wasn't the same once he and Martina parted ways. Besides that, Martina had walked out on him. Bitterness didn't begin to describe his feelings regarding her behavior back then.

The door chimed again, and his head jerked up. No Martina.

"I haven't seen you in here for a while Senator Kendricks," one of the shop's longtime employees said. "Welcome back. Can I top off that coffee for you?"

Paul smiled at the cheerful, grandmotherly woman who always had a kind word for anyone who entered Java Café. The coffee shop didn't have a wait staff, but she floated around the space greeting customers and offering refills as if they did.

"No thanks. I'm good."

"All right. Just let me know if I can get you anything."

Paul's cell phone vibrated in his pocket just as the woman walked away. He glanced at the screen and grimaced seeing that it was Davion.

Paul was still kicking himself for agreeing to go on a double date with Davion and his girlfriend. He should have known better. Not only couldn't Paul bring himself to call the woman by her name, but talking to her was like talking to a bowl of grits.

"You have the nerve to call me after that mess you pulled last night." Paul greeted. He ignored his cousin's burst of laughter through the phone line.

"I'm sorry, man." Davion finally said between chuckles. "I had no idea she had the intelligence of a two-year-old. You get big props for not just walking out of the restaurant when she asked if your job had anything to do with approving new perfume scents."

On that, Paul had to laugh. He'd had his share of bad dates, but never had he experienced anything like that before.

"Spending time with *Peppermint* last night makes

me want to propose a bill to quadruple the amount of money allocated to education. How did she make it through grade school, let alone graduate from high school talking like that?"

"I know. It would have served you right for me to intentionally hook you up with an airhead after your behavior yesterday morning, but I honestly had no idea she had the intelligence of a dodo bird."

"No harm done."

The mention of yesterday morning immediately brought with it thoughts of Martina. Paul hadn't slept well the night before thanks to dreams of her only proving what he now knew for sure. He wasn't over Martina Jenkins.

"So where are you? Normally, when you're in town on a Sunday morning, I smell bacon and eggs when I'm standing outside of your apartment door. Yet, here I am in the hallway and the smell of breakfast is nonexistent."

"I had to take care of something this morning and decided to just grab a quick bite at a coffee shop."

"Well the next time you decide to change the routine, tell somebody," Davion grumbled.

"Hey, it's not my fault you didn't call first. I do have other activities going on in my life besides making you breakfast."

"Yeah, whatever. You haven't had a life in a long time. I don't know why you suddenly…. Wait a minute. Does your missing in action have anything to do with the cutie pie carpenter?"

Paul groaned and sat back in his seat. He had hoped his cousin had forgotten about Martina. He should have known better.

"Tell me more about this carpenter. She must be

pretty special."

"It's a long story."

"I've got time, especially since I have to find me some breakfast."

*

Martina sat in the parking lot of her once favorite coffee shop, staring out the front window of her truck. She had survived the interrogation from Peyton and the others the night before, barely, but trying not to think about Paul had been a lost cause. Seeing him yesterday, had conjured up memories. Like how they used to meet at the coffee shop whenever he was in Cincinnati and she was on her way to work. Those first few weeks of getting to know him had been fun and exciting. And their relationship had taken off quicker than she had expected or wanted.

So much for expectations.

Paul had ruined her for any other man. She had gone out a few times with different guys since him, but rarely did she allow a second or third date. No one held her interest like Paul, and she knew none of them would have been able to please her sexually ... not like Paul.

Heat rushed through her body as she recalled some of their sexual escapades. In the closet, on the kitchen counter and on the balcony of his apartment were a few of their most memorable times together.

Martina shook her head to free the thoughts.

This has to stop. She couldn't keep dwelling on the past.

She climbed out of the white pickup truck, slamming the door shut. The dilapidated vehicle shook, and she cringed. Soon she would have to break down and invest in another mode of transportation.

Martina stood outside the glass door of the coffee shop, still debating on whether or not to go in. This was where she and Paul first met one chilly fall morning. She remembered the day as if it were yesterday.

Martina and two other carpenters had been working on a duplex in the area and stopped in during their afternoon break. That's when the most gorgeous specimen, with smooth chocolate skin, adorable freckles across his nose and cheeks, with lips so tempting she had almost made a complete fool of herself and kissed him. Thankfully, her coworker called her name, making her realize that she'd been staring at the man who she later learned was Senator Paul Kendricks.

Apparently, she hadn't been the only one looking. Paul waited near the entrance, stopping her on her way out to introduce himself. They did the typical small talk, and before she left the coffee shop, he asked for her telephone number.

Not only hadn't she given him hers, but she didn't accept his either. Not that she wasn't interested. On the contrary. The erotic feelings he stirred within her with his smile, hypnotic voice and interesting conversation, had her ready to drop her panties for him. Even his arrogance, claiming they would meet again, was a turn on.

"Here, let me get that for you, beautiful." A deep voice from behind startled Martina out of her reverie.

"Oh. Thanks."

She stepped in when the man pulled the door open, his overpowering cologne made her gasp, literally. It wasn't that he smelled bad, but it was as if he'd gone swimming in the stuff ... with his clothes on.

Martina thanked him again and entered the cozy café, doing a quick glance around. Why was she thinking she might see Paul? It had been a long time since she had visited Java Café on a Sunday morning.

This is a bad idea. What was I thinking coming here?

Martina knew exactly what she was thinking. She'd been thinking that just maybe the man who owned the most dazzling brown eyes and plumped lips that she missed kissing would be there.

You can keep lying to me if you want, but why are you lying to yourself? Peyton's words taunted her.

Martina stepped into the shortest line. She was accustomed to men approaching her, especially working construction, but today there was only one man she wouldn't mind running into.

She shook her head. No, the last person she needed to see was Paul Kendricks.

Martina surveyed the items in the glass display case, hoping they still carried the cranberry walnut muffins. Maybe she would get it to go. Eating there was bound to have her remembering a past that she really should leave buried.

*

Paul thought he might be seeing things. His heart lurched in his chest when he saw Martina enter the coffee shop with a tall, built man. Relief flooded through him like a warm breeze when he realized they weren't together. The idea of her with another man made him want to rip something apart.

She glanced around as if looking for someone and he wondered if maybe, just maybe, she was hoping to see him.

"Davion, let me call you back." Paul disconnected the call without giving his cousin a chance to respond. Leaving his jacket and magazine at the table, he headed her way just as she stepped up to the counter.

"Good morning. What can I get for you?" the perky brunette behind the counter asked Martina.

Before Martina could give her order, Paul jumped in. "She'll have a cranberry walnut muffin, steel cut oatmeal with brown sugar on the side, a fruit cup, and a venti caramel macchiato."

"I can place my own or—"

"And I'll have another black coffee and why don't you throw in a slice of the coffee cake."

Martina mumbled, but Paul couldn't make out what she was saying. That was probably for the best. He had been on the receiving end of enough of her rants.

The brunette's amused gaze darted between him and Martina. "Will there be anything else?"

"No that's it." Paul paid for the order and gently gripped Martina's elbow to guide her to where they would pick up breakfast. Surprisingly she didn't jerk out of his grasp when he didn't release her right away.

"I hate when you do that," she finally spoke. "I'm capable of ordering for myself. Besides, for all you know I might not have wanted what you ordered."

"Hello, Martina." Paul couldn't stop the smile that found its way to his mouth. "So, were you going to order something different?"

She narrowed her eyes at him. "That's beside the point!"

He chuckled. God, he missed this woman. Davion had asked the day before, why if Martina had such a big mouth, he'd want to get with her again. Paul knew

34

that behind that big mouth of hers was a kind, generous, loving woman who would give her last dollar to someone in need.

"Number fifty-four," the server called out.

Paul glanced at the receipt. *Fifty-six.*

"Why are you here anyway?" Martina pushed a long, wayward curl from her face only to have it return to the same spot.

He reached out before thinking and tucked it behind her ear, letting the back of his fingers glide down the softness of her cheek.

Interesting. She didn't push his hand away. Maybe this was a new and gentler Martina Jenkins. He could get used to this calmer side of her.

She pulled away as if suddenly remembering that she had dubbed him the enemy.

"You no longer have the right to touch me." She spoke through gritted teeth as she jabbed a finger into his chest.

This time, he laughed out loud.

Okay, so much for being gentler and kinder.

He grabbed hold of her finger and brought it to his lips.

"Ah, my sweet Martina. I was hoping you'd be here."

CHAPTER FIVE

Their gazes met, and Martina gulped. Tingles scurried up her arm and ricocheted through her body like fireworks exploding. Her heart pounded in her chest as Paul's skillful tongue swirled around the tip of her finger.

Groaning inside, she squeezed her thighs together trying like hell to tamp down the blast of heat that shot straight to her core.

Damn that was sexy.

He held her gaze as if willing her to have an orgasm right then and there. Damn if she hadn't come close.

The bastard.

He knew what he was doing. He knew that where he was concerned, it didn't take much to make her come.

Martina slowly pulled her hand from his grasp, wiping it down the side of her jean-clad thigh. Regaining her composure, she released the breath that had stalled in her chest.

"You were saying?"

Crap. What was I saying?

She narrowed her eyes when a stupid smirk spread across his handsome face. Frustration radiated through her pores. He still had the ability to distract her. What was it about this man that he could throw her off her game with little or no effort? What was he doing there anyway? Sure she had hoped to see him, but she didn't think she actually would.

"What, nothing to say? That has to be a first," he cracked.

Not waiting for a response, Paul stepped over to a nearby console that held napkins, straws, and condiments. Martina took the opportunity to check him out.

Male perfection.

The light-blue Henley shirt, stretched across his back, hugged his broad shoulders and thick arms. He might have spent many of his days sitting at a desk or meeting with constituents, but it was clear he still made time for working out.

Her gaze went lower to his tight butt and long legs covered by dark jeans. He resembled a high-powered attorney when he wore suits, but in casual wear, he had a *hot* bad boy thing going on.

Paul turned, catching her checking him out. The left side of his magnificent mouth tilted up into a smile. Martina had darn near melted to the floor when he came out of nowhere and ordered her breakfast. But now, those intense dark eyes, luscious lips, and sexy smile had her trying to hold herself together.

"So do you still come here often?" he asked.

"Not anymore." *Not since we parted ways* she wanted to add, but didn't.

She didn't bother looking up at him, at least not until she knew she was back in control of her faculties. What were the chances that they would both be at the coffee shop, where it all started, at the same time?

"Number fifty-six."

"That's us. I'll grab our meal. I'm sitting over—"

"I'm not staying," Martina blurted, surprising herself and catching the attention of those closest to them. There was no way she could endure being close to him much longer. She needed time to regroup … away from him.

Paul stopped and studied her for a moment, but didn't respond. He moved to the counter and grabbed their order.

"Come on. Sit and talk with me for a minute." He headed to the rear of the coffee shop without looking back, as if knowing she would follow.

"I should just walk out," she mumbled. "It would serve him right for thinking he can just boss me around."

Realizing she was standing there like an idiot talking to herself, she huffed and marched after him.

"You have a lot of nerve," she snapped when he stopped at the last booth. "First ordering for me and then assuming that I would sit and have breakfast with you. I'm not one of your little butt kissing lackeys. You can't just snap your fingers and think I will bow to your will."

Paul placed the food and drinks on the table before turning to her with a calm that pissed her off more.

"You're right. I'm sorry. I guess I was just surprised to see you in here, though I had hoped to run into you." He brushed a lock of curls from her forehead and reached for her hand, weakening her defenses. "Would you please join me for breakfast?"

A hopeful glint shown in his eyes and she felt like a spoil brat at her mini-tirade. What was wrong with her? Why did his presence stir up such craziness within her?

"Come on. You can give me a hard time after you eat." He topped his comment off with a legendary smile. He knew she couldn't resist that smile…or food.

Martina's family teased her about her hearty appetite, but not Paul. He fed her, claiming he loved a woman who enjoyed food as much as he did.

"Oh all right. I'll eat with you."

Once she sat across from him, the small talk felt forced, but then conversation flowed between them. They were both careful not to bring up any topics that would set either of them off. Namely – politics or their past relationship.

"So do you still cook?" she asked. The meals he often prepared were worthy of a fine dining establishment.

"Not as much as I used to," he answered, seeming to want to say more when he opened his mouth to speak again, but quickly closed it.

She hoped she wasn't the cause of him not cooking. Someone with his culinary talent really should be a professional chef. Not wasting his time on Capitol Hill passing ridiculous laws.

"So how have you've been, Martina?"

God the lyrical way he said her name, with that deep, sexy, baritone voice, sent goosebumps down her arms. Add that to the fact that she was sitting close enough to get a whiff of his fresh scent of spice and soap, so uniquely him, and she was ready to crawl into his lap.

She lowered her eyes. *Get it together girl.*

She brought her coffee cup to her mouth but didn't drink from it. "I've been all right. What about you? Besides talking crazy about unions to anyone who will listen, what have you been up to this past year?"

Paul chuckled, and she smiled behind the coffee cup. Now she was just teasing him. She liked some of his other political ideas. He was all for the state contributing more to funds that helped with homelessness and feeding the hungry.

"Same ol' same ol'. Traveling back and forth from Ohio to D.C. Seems I've been attending more events than ever this year, barely able to keep up with myself. I guess I'm just riding out this last year of my term, trying to decide what I want to do with the rest of my life."

"I hear you're thinking about running for president."

"That's just a rumor…probably started by my parents."

The bitterness in his tone told her he still wasn't interested in the job. He didn't want to be in politics. He had always felt a sense of obligation and as a third generation U.S. Senator, his parents felt that he was the family's best chance of adding a United States President to the Kendricks family legacy.

Martina never understood why, at forty, he just didn't tell his parents to take a flying leap instead of tolerating their nagging. She had never met the illustrious Kendricks, who came from old money.

They were well-known in Cincinnati for their philanthropy. It wasn't that Paul hadn't wanted her to meet them, on the contrary. He'd tried a few times to get her in front of his parents. She just wasn't having it. She knew how things like that worked. First meeting the parents, and then walking down the aisle to marry him. Nope, wasn't going to happen.

Martina had vowed years ago never to do something stupid like fall in love. She had watched her mother go through the vicious cycle of love and loss. With two failed marriages, Carolyn Jenkins still hadn't gotten it right. Martina had no intention of following in her footsteps.

"I know you don't want to hear this," Paul said interrupting her thoughts, "but it's good seeing you. You're as beautiful as ever."

Martina lowered her eyes to the oatmeal in front of her, feeling her face flame. She had received her share of whistles, compliments, and even cheesy pickup lines from men. It was different when Paul paid her a compliment. With him, it just felt different. Real. She knew his words were sincere and weren't just spoken to get into her panties.

After practically stirring the oatmeal to death, she finally chanced a glance at him. Her heart flipped. Desire radiated in his eyes as his gaze studied her.

"Thank you."

A sudden bout of nervousness crept through her body. This was ridiculous. She never got anxious. Maybe it was because she couldn't believe she was there with him. Well, technically, she wasn't with him. They just happen to be at the same spot, she told herself.

Between bites, Martina asked, "So how is Charlie?"

Paul's dog, a collie mix that he rescued two months before they met, had her thinking about getting a puppy.

Paul finished the coffee cake and wiped his mouth. "Charlie's great. My sister and her husband keep him when I'm in D.C. or traveling around the state. Leaving him at a kennel so often wasn't working out. I'm pretty much sharing the dog with them and my nieces, who are spoiling him rotten."

"That's nice. I think every child should have a pet." One of the activities that she and Paul enjoyed while dating was volunteering at one of the city's dog shelters. It was a wonder neither of them had a house full of dogs since they fell in love with some of the animals each time they volunteered.

"I've missed you," Paul said. He'd spoken the words so low, Martina wasn't sure if he had meant for her to hear him.

She didn't respond. She couldn't. If she opened her mouth, her brave front of no longer being interested in him would fly right out the window. She didn't want him to know how much she missed talking with him. How much she missed being in his arms, or how much she missed making love to him. Nope, some things were best left unsaid.

Paul leaned forward. His large hands, her weakness, folded around the coffee cup and he slowly lifted it to his sinfully sexy mouth. Unable to tear her gaze away, Martina sat mesmerized as he took a careful sip.

Their eyes met.

She gulped.

God she hoped he couldn't read minds. If he could, he would know that she wished that sinfully sexy mouth and those powerful hands were on her body making it come to life. Like before when those hands caressed her, paying extra attention to her breasts. Or when he would tweak her nipples, kneading them into perky pebbles. Her pulse kicked up just remembering how he would take one into his hot skillful mouth, swirl his tongue around the tip while teasing the other. And then…"

"What?" he asked.

Martina blinked.

A smile pulled at his lips as if he really could read her mind.

Martina blinked again feeling her face heat.

Paul sat back, his dark eyebrows now slanted downward. "Why are you looking at me that way?"

She didn't dare ask – what way. She knew. She knew that everything she once felt for him showed on her face. And she knew if she sat there too much longer she was going to say something stupid like *my place or yours.*

Desire hummed through her body, nipping at every nerve. She quickly glanced away.

What was I thinking coming here?

"Martina?" He covered her hand with his. "What's wrong?"

"I…I… Nothing," she murmured, willing her pounding heart to slow its rapid pace. If being in his presence for a half an hour had this effect on her, what did that say about her?

You are nothing like your mother. Peyton's words came back to her, but Martina knew. She knew that when it came to men, she was exactly like her mother.

No. No. I am not my mother. I am not my mother.

The silent chant looped through her brain over

and over again until she felt more in control. No way would she let a man, any man, reduce her to acting like some bumbling fool.

*

Paul stared across the table with concern at the woman who had stolen his heart a year ago. He didn't know why she'd spaced out, but it now seemed as if she was coming back to herself.

Studying Martina, she was such a contradiction. She had the face of an angel, a body of a goddess and the mouth of a bad-ass. Martina was passionate about everything from food to animals, to sex, and was stubborn as hell. She could be sweet as apple pie one minute and then turn around and curse you out, the next.

There was no other place he would rather be than in her company. Yes, maybe he was crazy. Maybe he was a glutton for punishment, or maybe he was just a man who was still in love with this amazingly complex woman.

"Now why are *you* looking at me like that? You said you wanted to talk, so talk."

In spite of himself, he chuckled. God, he missed her sass.

"What was really going on the night you walked out on me?"

"You know why I left." She stared down at the half-eaten muffin, surprising Paul. Martina always made eye contact. This shy, quiet woman sitting in front of him caught him off guard.

"At first, I thought you left because you were fed up with us arguing about my political platform, but now I'm not sure." He also had a feeling she'd left because he blurted out – I love you – in the heat of passion, but he wasn't positive.

She glanced up, searched his eyes before speaking. "My leaving couldn't have bothered you too much since you didn't come after me."

Hold up. Wait. What? Is that what she wanted? For me to go after her?

"Martina, your exact words were 'I'm done. Don't call me. Don't come by my house. Lose my damn number.'"

"Why can't you call me MJ like everyone else?"

"As I told you before, the name is as beautiful as you are and I have no intention of ever calling you anything but *Martina*."

Paul expected a smart retort, but one never came. Instead, she finished off her muffin as if they weren't just in the middle of a conversation. For the life of him, he had no idea where she put all the food she consumed. She could out eat most men he knew, yet at 5'5", she couldn't weigh more than a hundred and twenty pounds.

"Did you want me to come after you that night?" he finally asked.

Again silence. Shock coursed through his veins at the realization that she had actually wanted him to chase after her.

"Baby, talk to me. Tell me what I did that was so wrong back then that you had to walk out on me."

"You didn't stick to our agreement."

"What agreement?"

She leaned in closer. "We agreed to be friends with benefits. Nothing more. Then you had to go getting all serious and…and stuff."

"The 'and stuff' is what? When I started asking you to be my date for various events? Or when I

45

asked you what you thought about us moving in together? Or is the 'and stuff' when I told you that I loved you?"

Her jaw tightened. "All of that goes against the agreement of friends with benefits!" she seethed. "You knew going in that I didn't want all of that love crap. We were having a good time until you had to go and ruin it."

"Martina, I don't know what to tell you, except you're irresistible." It was the first thing that came to mind. "I didn't plan to fall in love with you. It just happened. Instead of you pushing me away, couldn't you just tell me how you felt?"

"I shouldn't have had to. You should have known."

"Let me ask you this. If I had taken some other woman to the events I invited you to, what would you have said?"

She shrugged. "Probably have a good time. Hell, I don't know. All I know is that my attending events and hanging out at your parent's palace weren't part of the agreement."

"So you would have been okay with me going out with someone else when you and I were together?"

Her lips twisted and frown deepened. "I wouldn't have cared."

"Like hell, you wouldn't have. Knowing you, not only would you have showed up and probably given the woman a verbal beat down, you would have cursed me out in the process."

After a long hesitation, she said, "Maybe, but we'll never know now will we?" Frustration roared through his body as she gathered up her handbag preparing to leave. "Well, we've talked. Now we can move on with our lives…separately."

"Hold up. You're just going to leave?"

"Yeah. We've eaten, talked, what else is there?"

He could think of a lot of things, like kiss and makeup. But he was pretty sure she didn't want to hear that.

"Martina, please sit down."

"Paul, it was great seeing you, but I have better things to do than sit around rehashing the past. Thanks for breakfast."

Martina turned to walk away, but he grabbed her hand. An electric charge shot up his arm and through his body. She shivered, and he had no doubt she felt it too.

Apparently, he was having more of an effect on her than she was letting on.

"Don't leave yet," he said close to her ear, still holding her hand.

She glanced down at their joined hands before her gaze met his. Those beautiful brown eyes that he'd seen over and over in his dreams held something he hadn't seen before. Vulnerability.

"Stay a little longer, or at least, have dinner with me tonight." He was preparing dinner for a local homeless shelter, but he'd find a way to have dinner with her as well.

"I…I can't," she said softly and eased her hand from his.

He looped his arm around her tiny waist, not letting her move away. Before she could protest, he lowered his head, and their lips touched. He had to find out if what he was feeling inside was mutual. He had to know if she still had feelings for him.

He nibbled at her top lip, then her lower one. She

parted her lips ever so slightly, inviting his tongue in for a taste.

Sweetness. She tasted even better than he remembered.

Her small hands slid slowly up his chest, and the softness of her lips against his had him holding her closer. They had probably garnered some attention. He didn't care. All he wanted was to continue holding her against his body, taking all that she was willing to give. But what he didn't want to do was scare her off. He wanted another chance with her plain and simple.

With one last peck, Paul lifted his head slightly. "I've missed you." The rasp of his voice carried the emotions jockeying around inside of him. "I—"

She pushed against his chest. "I'm sorry. This can't happen. I have to go."

She pulled out of his grasp, but not before he saw the sadness in her eyes. Something he had never seen before.

"Martina wait." He reached for her, but she dodged him, hurrying out of the building as if being chased.

A sigh slipped through Paul's lips. He ran a frustrated hand over his head and swore under his breath.

I don't know what's going on with you Martina Jenkins, but I have every intention of finding out.

*

Stupid, stupid, stupid.

Martina hurried to her truck, unable to get in fast enough.

What had she been thinking? And how the hell had she let him shake her like that? And that kiss…

Stupid, stupid, stupid.

Clearly she wasn't over him. She just wanted to believe she was. She hoped that she was. But nope. She still had it bad for the junior senator from Ohio.

Martina laid her head against the steering wheel, her heart racing like an express train. She had no respect for women who allowed a man to make them lose all common sense. She had made a conscious decision years ago not to be one of them. However, here she was falling under a man's spell because of a kiss.

How could she have let him kiss her? His kisses were like kryptonite. Yet, she allowed those enticing lips to touch hers. Had he not pulled back, there was no telling how long they would have remained in that lip lock.

"Ugh!" She screamed, pounding her hand on the steering wheel. She sat up straighter. "That's it. I'm done. I'm not going to keep subjecting myself to this nonsense. I am a grown, intelligent woman capable of saying no to a man."

Martina repeated those words to herself several times. After a few deep breaths, she glanced around the parking lot, glad that Paul hadn't run after her.

How had she let any of this happen? She wasn't supposed to fall for any man. All the years of keeping men at a distance should have prepared her for Paul.

She shoved her key into the ignition and started the truck, finally feeling sane enough to drive. She'd had a momentary slip. No more crazy thoughts about his eyes, mouth, or the way he could make her melt with just a kiss. From now on, she was staying away from romantic relationships. And most importantly, she was staying away from the likes of Senator Paul Kendricks.

CHAPTER SIX

Paul drove his Escalade up the winding hill of the residential neighborhood of Mt. Adams. Toward the home his grandfather had left him in his will. Melancholy settled in his chest remembering the man who had taught him practically everything he knew. From how to cook, to how to win a debate, Paul owed so much to his grandfather.

He crept up the street, already appreciating the scenic views that overlooked Cincinnati. He had been to the house only twice since his grandfather's passing, six months earlier. Until recently, he hadn't been sure what he wanted to do with the home. The only thing he knew for sure was that he would never sell.

Seconds after parking his truck in front of the three car attached garage, Davion pulled up alongside him.

"So why are we here?" Davion asked as they walked up the concrete stairs to the house.

"I'll tell you once we get inside."

Paul turned on a few lights, illuminating the wide, open space. His grandparents had lived in the home only a few years before his grandmother died. That had been ten years earlier. Once she was gone, his grandfather didn't stay in the house, saying that it wasn't a home without his beloved Constance. He also refused to sell the place.

"Okay, so what's going on?" Davion strolled into the outdated kitchen and leaned against the counter, his arms folded across his chest. "Are you planning to finally move in here?"

"I'm thinking about it." Paul stood at the floor to ceiling windows in the living room, the panoramic view of the river and the city sparkling below. The million dollar views were his favorite feature of the house.

He turned and did a cursory glance over the living and dining room. The open floor plan allowed him to also see into the kitchen. The place had such potential, and it was time he turned the home into the gem he envisioned.

"I want to hire Jenkins & Sons Construction to update the first and second floors before I move in." The first floor needed the most work, especially the kitchen, whereas the second floor was mostly cosmetic.

Davion's brows rose, and the left corner of his lips turned upward.

"Isn't that the company where the carpenter, who went off on you a few days ago, works? Didn't you say her family owns the business?"

Paul sighed and ran his hand over his head. "Yeah. It is."

Davion laughed. "So of all the construction

companies to hire, why that one? Why would you want a group of people who hate you, working on your house?"

"They don't hate me."

From what Paul had heard of Steven Jenkins, Martina's grandfather who started the company, Jenkins & Sons had the reputation of being the best in the business.

"Okay, well we know one of them hates you. As a matter of fact, I think she referred to you as the lowest form of human life." Davion laughed.

Paul couldn't stop his smile from appearing. He had seen Martina heated on a number of occasions, but that Saturday she had been livid. Yet, he knew she didn't hate him.

"I need you to do me a favor," Paul said to Davion. "I want you to call Jenkins & Sons and hire them to do the work on this house."

"Why can't you call?" his cousin asked, but realization showed on his face as he moved into the living room, standing in front of Paul. "Let me guess. You want the cute little firecracker, I mean *Martina,* to work on the house."

"Exactly. Since most of the renovations will require a carpenter, I want her. The only way we'll go with the company, is if Martina is the carpenter and oversees the job."

Davion shook his head and chuckled. "Why? The woman has made it clear that she can't stand you."

"Because she's the best damn carpenter in the city. Our political views might be different, but I know for a fact that her carpentry skills are top-notched, and I want the best on this project."

"No, you want her back in your life. What I don't

understand is why you need me?"

"I'm not sure how Martina would respond if I called and hired the company. She's second in command there and I don't want to give her any reason not to take on the job." Actually, he knew exactly how she would respond if he called directly. First, she would accuse him of playing some type of game and then she would assign another carpenter to the job. But he needed her to see the house and renovate it, knowing she would fall in love with the place. Which is what he wanted.

"So what? You want me to pretend this is my house? And what if she saw me with you that Saturday at the hotel?"

"No, you don't have to pretend this is your house, and where you were sitting in the banquet room that morning, I doubt if she saw you. Besides, she was too busy glaring at me. Anyway, I want you to be the go-to person. If asked, you can assure them that you can make all decisions for the owner. Oh and I want you to take any suggestions Martina gives regarding the house."

"You're going to put that much trust in this woman?"

"She won't steer you wrong. She might be a hothead, but she's very serious about her work. I'd like for them to start working as early as next week if possible. I'll be in D.C. off and on for the next month. So if asked, you can just say the owner is out of town."

"Okay, whatever you want, man. Just tell me what you want me to do. If there's a chance for you to get your woman back, the least I can do is help."

His woman.

Martina wasn't into labels, but what she had been at one time, was *his woman*. This idea was a little underhanded, and she was going to have a fit when she found out she had renovated a home for him, but he really did think she was the best.

"All right. Let me use the bathroom and then you can tell me what you want to do to the place. Oh and for the record, I think it's a dumb idea to deceive her. This ain't you, man."

Yes, his planned seemed a little deceptive, but Martina left him no choice. She wasn't returning his calls, not even the messages he had left at her job. Her cousins, Peyton and Toni, had assured him the messages were delivered. Martina ignoring Paul led him to stoop to such measures.

It was way past time they talked – really talk – without her running away from him. He shouldn't have waited this long, but prior to seeing her two weeks ago at the hotel, he thought he had moved on. However when he sat and talked with her at the coffee shop, he knew he hadn't.

Paul couldn't understand how he had allowed himself to fall for such a difficult woman. But if he were honest, he would have to admit that she was a complicated mix of sugar and spice. Exactly what he liked.

"There you go again, staring off into space. You've been doing that a lot lately," Davion said when he walked back into the front room. "Show me all that you want *your woman* to take care of."

He and Davion walked through the 4000 square foot home as he explained his ideas. For the first time since finding out his grandfather had left him the house, Paul was looking forward to the renovations.

What he wasn't looking forward to was coming face to face with Martina when she found out he owned the home.

"Something I don't understand," Davion started as they returned to the first floor. "Why would you want to be with a woman who's not interested in marriage and having a family when you know that's what you want?"

Two years earlier, when Paul had turned thirty-eight, he had started thinking more about settling down and having a family. It wasn't until he and Martina dated that he felt he finally found someone he could spend the rest of his life with. She was easy to talk to, most days, and they had fun together. She challenged him like no other, making him a better man. The more time he spent with her, the more he saw her as being perfect for him.

"I honestly don't know if she doesn't want to get married and have a family. Or if, for some reason, she's afraid of the idea. But I won't get a chance to find out if I don't convince her to talk to me."

Paul was ready for the next chapter in his life, and whenever he thought of the future, he saw Martina in his plans. He wanted her back. And he intended to have her. All he needed to do was find out what she had against being in a committed, life-long relationship.

*

Martina grabbed her bucket of tools from the back of the work van and sat it on the ground. She preferred driving her personal vehicle to jobs, but she didn't think the little Chevy pickup could handle the daily forty-five-minute commute this latest job required. The distance wasn't so much of a concern as was the narrow, winding streets that went up hill. She loved her little truck, but the last thing she needed was for it to stall out.

Her apprentice, Blaine, parked on the side of the van. A recent high school graduate, he had started with the company a few months ago, but this was the first time he worked with Martina.

He removed his tool belt from his trunk.

"Hey, MJ."

"What's up, kid?"

"Not much."

"God I love this house," she said as they strolled up the front walkway. They stood in front of the house and stared out over the city of Cincinnati below.

"You've said that every day for the past few weeks." Blaine shielded his eyes from the bright sunlight.

"I know. I know. I need to soak it all up since we only have about another week before this job is done." It had been awhile since she had been assigned a project that she looked forward to. There was nothing in the world she would rather do than carpentry work, but not all jobs were created equal.

They walked into the house and oddly enough, Martina felt as if she were arriving home. The same sense of peace had washed over her when she arrived there four weeks ago and had intensified each day after.

She and Blaine carried their tools into the kitchen and set them on a small piece of cardboard near the door that led to the back deck. Martina glanced around, pleased with how the space was shaping up. The antique gray cabinets had been installed, and the appliances were delivered three days ago. All they had left to do in the kitchen was to finish installing the hardware for the cabinets.

"It's been cool to help with the renovations on this place," Blaine said leaning against the sink counter, his hands shoved into the front pockets of his baggy jeans. "Thanks for letting me work with you. It's been a good experience."

"No problem, I'm glad you think so. Usually, Peyton assigns third-year apprentices to the jobs like this, so you lucked out."

"She said you requested me."

Martina smiled as she set the hardware for the cabinet doors on the counter next to Blaine. "I did request you." Though she hadn't planned on telling him. "I've watched you work, and I think you have potential. I wanted to see firsthand what you could do, and I must admit, I'm impressed. You did good kid."

Blaine grinned as if she had just offered him a million dollars. "Thanks! I've wanted to work with you, but I thought you didn't work with newbies."

"I made an exception."

Martina was picky about who she worked with since she usually took on the company's special projects and top priority jobs. She chose apprentices who already had a few years of on-the-job training, but Blaine stood out. Not because he was over six feet tall and lanky, but because of his eagerness to jump in and get his hands dirty.

They had gotten along from day one. He laughed at her antics and wasn't bothered by her dry sense of humor. She also appreciated that he didn't shrink under pressure or during those times when she got a little tough about doing things right the first time.

"Okay, shall we get to work?" she asked.

"Definitely."

Once Martina got Blaine started with the cabinet doors and hardware, she glanced around the kitchen. The space wasn't overly large, but one side opened into the great room, making the area feel like one large room.

Martina ran her hand over the granite slab sitting atop of the custom-made island she had built herself. When she suggested to the owner's friend, Davion, that she could build the perfect island for the space, he'd told her to go for it. As a matter of fact, he seemed willing to accept all of her ideas. Occasionally they had clients who were eager for their opinion, but they were so far in between until Martina had forgotten how good it felt to use her creative liberties on a job.

I guess I should get some work done.

On her way to the front of the house, she stopped at the far end of the great room to finish installing the crown moldings. The view outside snagged her attention. Whoever had designed the home was brilliant in putting the wall-to-wall windows at the front and the side of the house, easily bringing the outdoors in. The spectacular scenery stopped her in her tracks periodically throughout each day, stirring up dreams of owning a place in Mt. Adams.

Martina sighed and set up her ladder. Even if she worked the rest of her life, she wouldn't be able to afford anything like the five bedroom, four bathroom home, but she could dream.

Two hours later, Martina noticed Christina coming up the walkway.

"Wow, they've already moved furniture in here," Christina said when she walked into the great room. She set her buckets on the tarp near the front entrance and pulled a large rubber band from the back pocket of her jeans. "When I was here four days ago this place was empty. Now look at it."

"I know, right?" Martina walked across the room to her cousin. "You were supposed to be here hours ago. What took so long?"

"Peyton asked my team to stop by the Landmark project to knock out a small job before coming out here. Everyone else should be arriving in a few minutes."

"Oh good." Martina pulled on one of her cousin's long curls. "I know you have this flower child, hippie thing going on," she pointed to Christina's big, curly hair and tie-dye T-shirt, "but don't you think it's time for a haircut?"

"Yep," Christina said, the rubber band dangling between her teeth as she wrestled her hair into a ponytail. "But I can't. Luke likes my hair just the way it is."

"What does the thug lawyer know? He's not the one who has to maintain that bush."

Christina rolled her eyes. "Whatever."

Martina had dubbed Christina's live-in boyfriend the thug lawyer because he had more swagger than any lawyer she'd ever met. As a defense attorney, he had recently moved to Cincinnati from New York looking for a slower life than the east coast offered. He was also there to build a life with Christina.

Once her cousin finished messing around with her hair, she grabbed the buckets and paintbrushes and walked farther into the home. "Seems the owner has expensive taste," Christina said of the furniture that had been delivered the day before.

"Yes he does. I like his style. The rich colors make the room pop."

Instead of a typical sofa and love seat in the great room, the owner went with four upholstered chairs surrounding a glass and wood coffee table arranged to encourage conversation. The other half of the long room was used as another sitting area. Clearly he planned to do a lot of entertaining.

Martina followed Christina up the stairs, but stepped into the room that would be used as a den. The large, plush furniture and a sixty-inch television mounted on the only solid wall was calling her name. She could just imagine herself camped out watching football games on Sundays.

"By the libidinous expression on your face, I guess you like the den," Christina said when they met in the hallway.

"I love the den, but chill with the stupid big words. You know I don't know what they mean."

"You could stand to build your vocabulary."

"My language is fine."

"I beg to differ. Using words like *crap, stuff, chill*, and *stupid* means your vocabulary is lacking."

Martina waved her off. "Yeah, whatever."

Months ago, Christina had started learning a new word a day and had since tortured everyone with words that most people rarely used.

"It's good Davion gave us a heads up that the owner wanted the den painted first. Otherwise, it would have been a pain to cover all of his furniture and equipment."

"I know," Christina agreed. "We should be able to

finish everything we have to do up here before the end of the week. Hopefully, more items won't be delivered before then."

"Hopefully. Are you able to start on the master bedroom and bathroom this morning? Davion mentioned that the owner would be back in town at the end of next week. Even if everything isn't totally done by then, let's make sure the most important spaces are completed."

"I agree. There'll be three painters here today, and Ben Jr. will be here in the next couple of days to help us knock everything out. I'll start in the master bedroom."

"Sounds good."

Martina followed her into the master suite and leaned against the doorjamb, her hands shoved into the back pockets of her dark jeans.

"I see you're still envisaging this place as your own," Christina commented.

Envisaging? Martina didn't bother asking what it meant, not wanting to encourage her to use more of those words.

"You have that wistful look on your face that you've been wearing for the last few days."

"Is it that noticeable?" Martina asked.

"Yep."

"Every time I walk in here, I think about that large soaking tub Toni and her crew installed the other day. If I had a bathroom like that, I would never leave home. The only thing missing is a big screen TV in front of the tub."

Christina laughed. They all knew how much Martina loved sports. Outside of having dinner with the family on Sundays, her weekends were usually filled with sitting in front of the television watching football or basketball. Now that it was football season that's all she thought about. Well, that and Paul.

The constant thoughts of him weren't plaguing her mind as much as they were a few weeks ago. But often enough. Since he had stopped calling, she felt that she had some of her control back. Though, she wasn't sure how she felt about him just disappearing again. Part of her was glad he had moved on. Yet, there was another part of her that missed him like crazy. Had it not been for that kiss—

"Don't you have work to do? Or are you ruminating about all that you could be doing with the handsome Senator, who shall remain nameless since I don't want you to go off on me."

Martina didn't embarrass easily, but she felt like crap the way she verbally attacked her cousins the day Paul kissed her. She had been thrown off kilter after leaving the coffee shop and still hadn't fully recovered when she attended Sunday brunch later that day at her grandparent's house. Her cousins immediately assumed her behavior had something to do with Paul.

"So?" Christina drew out the word, pulling Martina back to the present.

"So you're right, about me having work to do. And on that note, I'm outta here. Oh and for the record. I was daydreaming about what it would be like to live here." It wasn't a total lie. Living in this home would be a dream come true.

"Uh huh," her cousin said unconvinced. "Well, get to work, but don't stop dreaming. This could be you one of these days."

"Ha! Yeah right."

CHAPTER SEVEN

The following week, Martina did a quick walk through of the Mt. Adams home. After a long day, they finally finished everything. Everyone else had left, but she was waiting for Davion to conduct the final walk through.

Martina stepped out onto the upper level back balcony, taking in the fresh air and gentle breeze that caressed her face. Her curls whipped around, and she pushed a few strands away from her eyes as she soaked in the last bit of paradise.

"One day I'm going to have something like this," she said quietly. All she had to do was stick to her financial plan and a home like this could be hers.

Martina turned when she heard a sound from the first floor. So caught up in her thoughts, she temporarily forgot she was waiting for Davion.

Martina re-entered the house and headed for the stairs, but slowed when she smelled food. The scent of barbecue eased up the staircase and had her mouth-watering with each step. She'd skipped lunch in an effort to get everything done on time, and her stomach had been growling for the past hour.

"Hello," she called out when she hit the bottom step but didn't see anyone.

She rounded the corner into the kitchen and gasped, her hand hovering over her chest.

"What the hell are you doing here?" Shock kept her rooted in place. "How did you get in?"

"I live here."

Paul loomed near the front door, his wide shoulders spanning the width of the doorway. Despite the initial shock of seeing him, butterflies fluttered around in her gut. The man was built more like a football linebacker than a U.S. Senator.

His last comment snapped her back to the issue at hand.

I live here.

He moved slowly toward her as she tried to process his words. Her mind conjured up every conversation she'd had with Davion throughout the project attempting to recall any clue to Paul's claim.

"Hello, Martina."

Damn that voice.

"Don't hello, Martina me. *You* own this place? You're the *friend* Davion kept referring to?" She continued to stare at Paul as she tried to wrap her brain around the fact that he owned this dream house. She knew he had done well reinvesting a portion of the trust fund he had received when he turned twenty-five, but she was stunned that he purchased this gem.

"Yes. I'm the owner."

Her brows drew together. "Why? Why would you—"

"Before you say anything else … or throw something at me, let me explain."

"You don't have to explain anything to me!" Martina headed to the door where she left her equipment. "The job is done, and I'm out of here. I don't have time to take part in whatever game you're running. I—"

"Wait." He grabbed hold of her hand just as she wrapped her fingers around the handle of the tool bucket, an electric current skittering up her arm. She wasn't surprised that his touch sent heat shooting through her body, but she ignored her body's reaction. All she wanted to do was get the heck out of there. "Just hear me out." Paul's voice was low and pleading. She had to admit she was curious as to why he felt a need to hide behind Davion to get this project done.

She noticed the insulated food carrier on a nearby table and a picnic basket in the hand that wasn't covering hers.

Paul set the basket on the table next to the other container. The scent of food reached her brain, and of course, her stomach chose that moment to growl.

"Why, Paul?"

"I know Jenkins & Sons is the best construction company in the city. And the fact that you are the best damn carpenter there is, it was a no-brainer. I had to hire your family's company."

He gestured for her to take a seat in the sitting area closest to the front door. After a slight hesitation, she moved to one of the chairs.

"I don't like games, Paul."

"I know, baby. I wasn't running a game. You left me no choice since you were avoiding my calls. It was either this," he waved his hands in the air gesturing around the room, "or sit outside your house every day and stalk you. And besides, I didn't want to risk you or your family declining my project."

"Well you clearly don't know the Jenkins family," she murmured and crossed her legs. "There's no way Peyton would let a job this size slip out of the company's hands. She might have assigned a different carpenter, but no way would she have turned it down."

The left corner of his lips lifted into a half smile. "Good to know. I'll keep that in mind."

"So was Peyton and Toni in on this ... this little charade or whatever you want to call it?"

Paul shook his head and sat across from her. "No."

For the first time since walking down the stairs, she took a good look at him. His eyes weren't as vibrant as usual, and the scruff on his cheek and chin were thicker than the last time she'd seen him. No doubt he was tired and knowing him, he had probably been putting in long hours, sacrificing sleep.

She shook her head and stood abruptly. His well-being wasn't her problem.

He stood as well. "Martina, please don't leave until we talk."

"Paul, we have nothing to talk about. Have you been in politics so long that now you're into deceiving people? Not caring who might get hurt in the process. A regular chip off the old block, huh?"

The moment the words were out of her mouth, she regretted them. A heatwave of shame traveled through her body.

"I'm sorry. That was uncalled for." She watched as

a range of emotions flitted across his face. She couldn't believe she'd said that to him. The last year of his father's term in the Senate had been overshadowed by a scandal. The senior Kendricks had lied about accepting donations from a foreign country. Instead of admitting his involvement, he let his intern take the fall. It wasn't until an investigation into the situation revealed that Paul Kendricks Sr. was behind the mess.

"That's even low for you," Paul finally said and put some distance between them. From day one of his Senate term, he worked his butt off to prove to the country that he was not his father.

"I'll admit I probably should have tried to get your attention a different way, but I would never deceive anyone to the point of someone getting hurt." As was the case with his father. Many people had lost their jobs.

"I know, and I really am sorry I said that. But why'd you lie? Why go through all of this?"

"I never lied about anything. My only deception is that I had Davion filling in for me."

He really hadn't done anything wrong. Davion lied about meeting her at the house tonight and as far as she knew, he hadn't lied about anything else.

"You know what, Paul? Before I say something else inappropriate, I'm leaving. I don't care why you felt a need to hide behind someone else to get your house renovated."

Actually, she really did care, but right now, being this close to him, she could barely think straight.

She grabbed her jacket from a hook near the door and lifted the pail of tools. Paul followed her out the door.

"Would you just calm down and wait?"

Martina stored the items in the back of the van and slammed the door.

"Wait for what? I don't like games, Paul. So—"

"Don't you?" He stepped in front of her, blocking her from climbing into the driver's seat. "You're the queen of games. I'd think something like this would be right up your alley."

Fury stirred in her gut. "I don't know what you're talking about, but you're about to piss me off. So trust me, it'll be best for both of us if I leave before I do something to you that I might or *might not* regret."

"Was any of it real, Martina? Or, was I just a means to satisfy your insatiable sexual appetite?"

That stopped her. She wasn't sure how to respond. The fury stirring inside of her only moments ago had quickly turned into something else. Frustration. Disappointment. Longing.

How could he even ask her that? He had to know how hard it was for her to walk away from him back then, but she had to. She had to protect herself. She had to protect her heart.

Staring at him now, she still wasn't sure how to respond without him thinking that she wanted them to try again. Sure she could admit that he was the only man who satisfied her completely. But no way would she admit that she had done something as stupid as fall in love with him.

She turned from the van but didn't close the driver's side door. "I cared about you, Paul, but we had an agreement."

"Oh yes, the agreement. What was it again?" He moved closer, invading her personal space. "That we would continue our secret affair with no strings attached? That we would agree *not* to fall in love even though we had so much in common, had the best conversations, enjoyed the same things, and had an incredible sex life? Is that the agreement you're speaking of?"

Martina sighed loudly. "Don't do this." She wasn't admitting anything, to anyone. She vowed years ago that she wouldn't fall into that vicious cycle that many women fell into. Meet a great guy. Have a good time. Fall in love. Get dumped. Then start all over again.

"Come back inside with me. We need to talk about what happened. Once and for all. *And* if you come inside, I'll tell you about the house… 'cause I know you're curious."

She heard the humor in his last comment, which she appreciated. No doubt the conversation wasn't over, but she welcomed his effort to lighten the moment. They had only known each other six months before their split, but he knew her. He knew her better than most. And he knew that she had an infatuation with homes, especially a home as spectacular as this one.

Martina pulled her bottom lip between her teeth trying to decide if sharing a meal with him was a good idea. But then her stomach betrayed her, rumbling so loud it interrupted the quietness outside.

"Come on. I know you're hungry after a long day of work. I made barbecue spare ribs, pasta salad, asparagus wrapped in bacon…"

Martina stopped listening after bacon. Unfortunately, he knew there was nothing she loved more than food, except for maybe sex and football.

"Oh and I think there are some chocolate chip walnut cookies in the basket." He slowly reached for her hand and squeezed. "Don't make me eat alone."

Between the hypnotic scent of his cologne, his gentle touch, and that smooth baritone voice that sent delicious shivers through her body at his last statement, she was about ready to follow him to the ends of the earth.

Her stomach rumbled again.

Paul smiled. "I assume that's a yes?"

"Don't be a smartass." She allowed him to lead her back into the house.

So much for maintaining control.

She shook the thought loose. She was an independent, intelligent, strong woman. Strong enough to still be in control and have dinner with him without falling for him again.

At least she hoped.

CHAPTER EIGHT

"Let's eat at the island."

Paul grabbed the food containers and followed her into the kitchen unable to stop checking out her backside. Besides Martina, there wasn't a woman alive who could make a pair of jeans look that good. He might have been tired, but the sight of her apple-shaped derriere was giving him renewed energy.

His gaze slid lower to her work boots, and a smile pulled at his lips. Those dirty, well-worn, sexy as hell steel-toe boots still had the ability to stir something erotic in him. He especially liked when she wore them with denim shorts.

He mentally slapped himself when a burst of lust shot through him, and he absently licked his lips. He needed to keep his head on straight. Getting her to stay for dinner was only half the battle. Now he wanted to find out what her real issue with commitment was about and convince her to give them another chance.

But he planned to take things slow with her this

time around. He wanted forever and knew he was going to have to tap into every bit of patience he had.

"By the way, the place looks great," Paul said when they sat at the kitchen island. The high back bar stools were perfect for the space.

"That's right, you haven't seen it…or have you?"

He hesitated. "I stopped by late one night. Maybe once we finish eating, you can give me the grand tour. I hear that you designed and built this island."

"Yeah and considering your deception, I should rip it out and let you sit on the floor. I should walk out that door and never look back."

"But you won't. At least not until you taste the ribs and everything else I made especially for you."

He pulled dishes out of the basket and by her silence, she wasn't going anywhere. At least not until she ate.

"Well, you're lucky I'm hungry. Besides, you owe me." She accepted the paper plate of food.

"I owe you for what?"

"For all the *extra* work I did around here. I added some special touches. You'll soon see my team and I outdid ourselves."

She bit into the rib. Lust swirled through his body, jumpstarting desire that had laid dormant since she walked out of his life. Watching her eat was an event in itself. Her eyes slid closed, and she groaned with pleasure. The sexy sounds soaked into his pores. It was taking everything within him not to pull her into his arms and devour her mouth.

"Good, huh?"

"Everything is delicious. I see you still have skills."

He chuckled. "And I'm glad to see you still have a healthy appetite. I love feeding you."

He took the fork from her, scooped up the baked beans, and held the utensil to her lips. Their gazes met, and something passed between them. Something he couldn't quite identify. Maybe awareness. Like him, she probably recalled how sharing a meal used to be between them.

After a long pause, Martina glanced at the fork laden with food and opened for him. The slow, sultry way her mouth slid over the fork was almost his undoing. His throat went dry, and his jeans suddenly felt a little too tight in a certain area.

Served him right for feeding her, knowing that watching her eat was a serious turn on.

He lowered the fork to the plate and stood.

"I'll be right back."

He headed for the front door, needing some air, a chance to pull himself together. Good thing he left a small cooler of drinks in his SUV. By the time he grabbed the drinks and sucked in a few cleansing breaths, he was ready to go back inside.

"You look exhausted," Martina said when he stepped back into the kitchen. As if on cue, he yawned.

"It's been a tough few weeks, and I haven't been sleeping well. I just got back in town a few hours ago." Paul stared down at all of the food on the counter. "I wanted to prepare dinner for you and bring it out here before you left."

"Your friend set me up. He better hope I don't run into him."

Paul laughed. "He's my cousin." And if things went according to Paul's plans, she would definitely see Davion again.

"So tell me about the house. What happened to

your downtown apartment? I thought you preferred apartment living since you spend half your time on the east coast."

"I still have it." He picked at the pasta salad on his plate while Martina finished off almost half her meal. He really couldn't talk about the place without discussing his hero. "My grandfather left me the house in his will. He died six months ago."

"Oh no. Paul, I'm sorry. I hadn't heard." Martina covered his hand with hers and warmth traveled through his body. "I know how close you two were."

He had often talked about his family, especially his parents who drove him nuts. Discussing family was something he did, but that wasn't the case with Martina. He knew her grandparents raised her and that she was close to her four female cousins, but her parents were a mystery to him.

"Some days I have to remind myself he's gone. I keep expecting to get a call from him telling me that I work too much. Or that he needs me back here in Cincinnati so that my parents can pick on me and leave him the hell alone." Paul chuckled, but the weariness he felt for his loss went deep.

"What happened?" Martina wiped her hands on the napkin he had placed next to her earlier. "Was he sick?"

"Pops had been diagnosed with congestive heart failure last year. His doctor tried putting him on a strict diet and convincing him to get more exercise, but the old man was stubborn. He loved food almost as much as you and I. Instead of taking his health serious, he insisted that no matter what he did, when it was his time to go, it was his time to go. He died of a massive heart attack."

"Oh, Paul, I really am sorry."

Paul shrugged. "Thanks. Pops was one of the good guys."

They sat in silence for a long stretch, each of them caught up in their thoughts.

"Sooo, I guess you have to deal with your parents by yourself now."

He chuckled. Her comment reminded him of the time he had told her that he would rather be stranded on a deserted island for a year than to be left alone with either of his parents for more than a day.

"Don't remind me. My grandfather is not around to come to my rescue when dealing with them, especially when they start discussing me running for president. Which I have no intention of doing, but they refuse to hear any of that. Anyway, the old man left a lot of great memories."

"I don't want to think about how it would be if I didn't have my grandparents in my life. They are my rock, especially my grandmother. When my mother…"

He waited, hoping she would continue. When she didn't, he prompted her. "When your mother what?"

She shook her head. "Nothing."

Paul decided not to push. She would open up to him one day. He just hoped it was sooner than later.

"So your grandfather left you the house months ago. Why'd you just decide to move in?"

He took a swig of his beer. "Because I ran into you."

Martina's eyebrows dipped. "What does that have to do with anything?"

"I wanted to see you again. Since you keep running from me, I figured I'd try a different tactic."

"Pretty expensive tactic don't you think?"

"Maybe, but it was worth every single penny to share a meal with you."

"You shared a meal with me a month ago. You didn't have to spend tens of thousands of dollars to have a meal with me, Paul. So what's the real reason for all of this?"

He shrugged, rubbing his head, exhaustion seeping deeper into his body. "At the time, I felt I was killing two birds with one shot. I was finally getting this place renovated, and it gave me a chance to see you again. I know it's a little extreme, but Martina there is nothing I wouldn't do to have you in my life again."

Martina sat speechless, fidgeting in her seat. Instead of responding, she went back to eating. He took her silence as a good sign. At least, she didn't take off. She knew as well as he knew that there was still a smoking hot connection between them. Paul wanted to explore that connection to see if he could turn it into something deeper. Something deeper that she wouldn't be able to deny.

He watched her eat and couldn't take it any longer.

"Don't do that," he practically growled.

Martina froze. "Don't do what?" She licked her lips, trying to get the barbecue sauce off her mouth.

"That."

He moved closer and placed a finger under her chin before lowering his head. Martina stiffened but didn't stop him. He licked the barbecue sauce that was near her mouth. From there he had to taste her.

Slipping his tongue between her slightly parted lips, arousal flared within him. Her mouth was just as inviting, her lips just as sweet as before. Kissing him back like this, Paul knew there was no way Martina didn't still have feelings for him.

As soon as the thought entered his mind, Martina ripped her lips from his. "Wait. I can't be kissing clients," she panted.

"Former client. I paid the balance two days ago." He stood, pulling her up with him.

Before Martina could respond, his lips covered hers again, and he folded her into his embrace, holding her tight. The initial hesitation vanished, and her arms slid around his neck.

Paul reveled in the way she fit perfectly against him and how her tongue dueled with his. Ripples of pleasure jockeyed around inside of him.

On a groan, his hands palmed her bottom. The feel of her ass in his grasp lit a flame that wouldn't be easily doused if he didn't slow down. He couldn't mess this up by taking things too far, and if they kept going like this, that's exactly what would happen.

He wanted forever. Not just a quick lay.

With strength he didn't realize he possessed, he pulled slightly away, but didn't drop his hands from her rear.

"God, I've missed you."

Her hand hovered over her mouth. "I…uh…I have to go."

Paul sighed and dropped his hands. "You can't keep running, Martina, when there is clearly something still between us."

"I'm not. Well not exactly." She quickly gathered her belongings. "I have to go to school. I have class tonight."

"Oh." He wasn't ready for her to leave, but at least this time she had a good reason.

Paul walked her outside while she told him he'd

have to give himself a tour. He wanted her to stay, but didn't want to make her late. He also didn't want to scare her away for good.

"I noticed you're rolling in the company's van. Does that mean you finally got rid of that piece of junk that you call *your baby*?" More times than he could count, he had offered to purchase her another vehicle for fear that old truck would break down, and she'd be stranded somewhere.

"I still have it, and she's still going strong...sort of. And I don't appreciate you talking about my baby."

Paul backed Martina against the van, blocking her in with his arms on each side of her, his hands flat against the van.

"Are you sure you have to leave?"

"Yes." She glanced at her watch. "As a matter of fact, if I don't hustle, I'm going to be late. Besides, you need to get some rest." She cupped his cheek and stared into his eyes. "Thank you for dinner. It was excellent."

"Does that mean you forgive me for not being totally honest about the house?"

She sighed dramatically. "I guess I forgive you, but just don't do it again."

"I won't. So if I call you sometime, will you answer?"

"Why?"

He pulled back slightly. "Martina, why do you always give me a hard time?"

"Because it's what I do. Besides, you like it when I give you a hard time. Be honest. Don't you?"

He smiled. "Maybe, but damn girl, can't you give a brotha a break sometime?"

She burst out laughing. Evidently, his hip-hop flow

wasn't hitting the mark.

"Okay, you can call me."

"And…"

"And I'll answer. But right now, I really have to go."

"I'm proud of you." The back of his fingers glided slowly down her cheek.

"Why?"

"Because of your determination to get your degree. I know it can't be easy working construction during the day and then attending night school."

"It's not easy, but it's something I have to do. After this semester, I'll need six more credits to complete the requirements for my business degree."

She had once told him that she planned to one day run Jenkins & Sons Construction. She and, Peyton, had discussed trying to expand the business to northern Ohio.

"I know you're going to do it. Let me know if there is anything I can do to help. I'm great in History and English. I'm also available if you need a mental break and maybe want to work off some pent of energy."

He wiggled his eyebrows, and she burst out laughing.

"Oh, I bet you can. I'll keep all of that in mind, but right now I have to get going." She said the words, but neither of them moved.

"Have dinner with me next Friday." Paul nuzzled her neck. He knew he was getting to her by the grip she had on the front of his shirt and the soft whimpering sounds she made as he laced her neck with feathery light kisses.

"I…I can't have dinner with the enemy," she

murmured.

Paul chuckled and slowly lifted his head. "Well technically, you just had dinner with me, *and* you kissed me as if we were no longer enemies."

She pushed against his chest, and he dropped his arms. "Well *technically*, you tricked me into having dinner with you. You knew I wouldn't be able to resist your barbecue ribs. So tonight doesn't count. And *you* kissed me. I only kissed you back because I didn't want to be rude."

Paul threw his head back and laughed. "You're a real piece of work."

"And you're still on my short list of enemies."

She folded her arms across her chest, and his gaze immediately settled on her breasts. She wasn't as top heavy as some of the women he'd dated in the past, but she was more than a handful. Add that to all of her other tempting assets and he could barely keep his hands off of her.

"So give me a chance to get my name off that list."

He wanted to see her again. Hell, he had to see her if he ever wanted to get a good night's sleep. Every waking hour for the last few weeks had been filled with thoughts of her.

He placed his hand on her hip and moved closer. "I'll tell you what. Since I don't want us to be enemies any longer, how about we get together over dinner next Friday and discuss, calmly, the situation regarding the unions?" He placed a finger against her lips when she started to speak. "That way you can give me some constructive ideas on how I might be able to turn this into a win-win for the state, as well as for the unions."

He dropped his hand, but she didn't speak right

away. Instead, she stared at him as if trying to decide if he were serious, or if he was trying to play her.

"Don't say no," he said. "This is a perfect opportunity for your concerns to be heard and an opportunity for us both to maybe get what we want."

He didn't bother adding that all he wanted at the moment was her. Their time apart did nothing to squelch his desire. Just being in her presence today made him long for her that much more.

And in all honesty, he really did want to hear her out about the unions.

"Okay, I'll think about it, but right now I'm outta here."

He kissed her one last time then held the door while she climbed into the van.

"I'll call you."

"I'll be waiting."

Paul would give her a few days, but if he didn't hear from her soon, she would be hearing from him. No way would he let her run again.

CHAPTER NINE

Paul sat in his D. C. office, elbows on the desk and his hands steepled. He impatiently listened as Senator Ted Collins droned on about the committee meeting they had just returned from.

"I'm telling you, Paul, we all need to come to some consensus soon regarding this gun control bill that the Democrats are trying to bring back to the table."

The first thing that morning Paul had gone to the Senate floor to debate a bill, followed by three back-to-back meetings. He wasn't in the mood to rehash the last meeting that consisted of mostly arguments.

Ted was all riled up over a bill Paul wasn't sure how he felt about. He respected the second amendment giving Americans the right to bear arms, but he also felt tougher laws needed to be in place.

"And what the heck was that all about with them trying to connect everything to mental health? I think they are reaching. We already stopped the gun control bill from passing last year. I know they…"

Paul tuned out. This time a vision of Martina with

barbecue sauce on the side of her mouth infiltrated his mind. It had been three days since their impromptu dinner, and he hadn't heard from her regarding the dinner invitation. Part of him thought she would call, but there was a part of him that wasn't so sure. She was the most unpredictable woman he knew. That was part of the appeal. She kept him guessing … and wanting more.

"They might be trying to reconfigure the bill," Ted's voice pulled him back to the present, "but as far as I'm concerned, I don't think we—"

Paul's cell phone vibrated on his desk.

"Excuse me, Ted."

Paul glanced at the screen where Martina's smiling face showed. "Ted, this is an important call I've been expecting. Maybe we can continue this discussion a little later."

"No problem. I'll catch up with you this evening."

Paul waited until Ted closed the door behind him before answering.

"Senator Kendricks."

"Senator Kendricks, this is Martina *"MJ"* Jenkins. I hope I'm not calling at a bad time."

Paul smiled despite himself at the sultriness of her voice. No doubt she was trying to get a rise out of him. And it worked.

"This is a pleasant surprise, Ms. Jenkins. To what do I owe the pleasure?" He really didn't care. Just hearing her voice had stirred something within him, and he was glad for the call. She could make his day by accepting his invitation to dinner.

"I've decided to take you up on that dinner offer this weekend … with a couple of conditions."

Paul sat back in his seat and sighed. He had a

feeling he wasn't going to like her conditions.

"Let's hear them."

"Okay first. No fancy restaurant. They don't put enough food on the plates. Second, I want you to take me seriously when I explain why the Governor's idea regarding the unions is a bad one. And third, none of that touchy feeling crap. You keep your hands and your lips to yourself. And lastly, you have to make me a batch of those Reese's Peanut Butter Cup cookies. I want at least twelve of them."

A smile spread across Paul's mouth. He heard the humor in her voice as she ticked off her demands and was glad she decided to go out with him. During their impromptu dinner at his house, though it started rocky, by the end of the night he felt that she had softened. Accepting his dinner invitation was a good sign.

"Anything else?" he asked.

She hesitated. "Nope. I think that's it."

"Okay deal, except, I can't guarantee I'll be able to keep my hands and my lips to myself. You're irresistible."

"Well, you'd better try unless you want to lose a hand."

Paul laughed at her quick comeback. There was never a dull moment with Martina and Friday night couldn't come fast enough.

*

Days later, Paul stepped across the threshold into Martina's small bungalow and almost didn't recognize the place. Not only had she installed siding on the outside of the structure, but she had totally transformed the interior. Walls had been removed, creating an open floor plan and now the living room, dining room, and kitchen were visible from the foyer.

She'd purchased the home shortly after they started dating against his better judgment. Though she was a master carpenter, he didn't think anyone should purchase a home where large, gaping holes in the walls were the first thing you noticed when you walked in.

"So what do you think?" Martina stood in the kitchen, returning a pitcher to the refrigerator. "Big difference, huh?"

"I'd say. It almost doesn't look like the same place. I knew you had skills, but this place looks fantastic."

"Thanks. I did the majority of the structural work and my cousin Jada came up with the color scheme and staged the rooms."

"She did a great job."

"Yeah, she's not only the fashionista in the family, but her interior decorating skills are second to none. I told her that once she finished fashion design school, she should use some of her design skills to stage homes for a living."

Paul made his way to the kitchen and stood across the counter from her. "So are all of you in school?"

She shook her head as she finished wiping down the counter. "No, just Jada and I. Peyton has a business degree, and Toni attended night school during her apprenticeship and she has an engineering degree. Oh, and Christina didn't go the college route. Have you ever heard of Sasha Knight?"

"Yes, I have one of her paintings at my apartment in D.C. Why do you ask?"

"That's Christina."

Paul's brows shot up. "Your cousin is *Sasha Knight*?"

Martina laughed, and the rich sound of her laughter wrapped around him like a warm embrace.

"Yep. So, when you say you have some of her work, do you have one of her nudes?"

Paul laughed. "No, it's an abstract painting. I had no idea she painted nudes."

"Neither did I," she snorted. "Our family just found out a few months ago that she not only is world famous, but she paints under an alias."

"I imagine your family was surprised by that revelation."

"Oh yeah. Very surprised." Martina walked around the counter. "Come on, I'll show you the rest of the house before we leave."

Paul followed behind her from room to room of the three-bedroom, two bathroom home. He tried to focus on what she was saying regarding the changes she had made, but he kept getting distracted. She looked great in the V-neck shirt that was tucked into fitted jeans. Jeans that hugged her tight butt like a second skin.

He followed her down the stairs to the basement where she created a rec room that would be the perfect man cave. "So what happens next now that you're almost finished renovating?" Paul asked at the end of the tour.

"It'll go on the market in a couple of weeks, and I'll start looking for another place to buy."

"What if this place sells before you find the next place?"

She shrugged. "I'll cross that bridge when I get to it."

Martina pulled a lightweight jacket from a closet near the front door, and Paul reached for it. He held it open as she slid her arms into the sleeves. The fresh, familiar scent of her perfume caught his attention and he inhaled. Instead of releasing her once she slipped into the jacket, he pulled her back against him.

"God, I've missed you."

"Same here, Senator." Martina turned in his arms and before he could utter another word, her lips covered his. During their recent make-out sessions, he'd been the initiator, but this ... this brought back memories of heated nights and sultry lovemaking. Martina wasn't shy and always took what she wanted. Paul had no doubt that if they ever ended up back between the sheets, the connection would be explosive.

He wasn't sure what changed in the last few days since she'd given him her lists of conditions, but he welcomed the change.

She felt good rubbed up against him. The kiss was unexpected but very much desired. He wanted more. Much more.

When the kiss ended, he linked their hands and pulled her to the door.

"We'd better get going before I forget that I'm a gentleman."

"I for one think being a gentleman is highly overrated sometimes," Martina said when they stepped onto the small porch, and she locked the door.

Instead of responding, Paul adjusted himself and appreciated the cool air, hoping it would tap down the yearning flowing through him.

"Thanks for coming out to dinner with me," Paul said once they were settled inside the car and were heading toward Mt. Adams. He planned to take her to a small cafe that he'd run across. Martina wasn't a woman who enjoyed five-star restaurants. No, she was a burger and beer type woman.

"I thought you were going to make me work a little harder before going out with me."

"Some things haven't changed that much. There's not much I wouldn't do for food."

Paul raised an eyebrow, but before he could speak, she continued.

"Don't go getting any ideas. I would do *almost* anything for food."

He chuckled. "I'll keep that in mind."

"So what's with the suit?" Martina asked.

Paul glanced down at his attire. He had tossed his tie into the backseat, hoping to look a little more casual.

"I came straight from the airport. My plane arrived a little later than expected."

"You know, we could have postponed dinner. I didn't realize you were just getting back in town."

"It's not a problem. I've been looking forward to seeing you all week."

Forty minutes later, he pulled up to the café. Considering how good the food was and how phenomenal the views were in the back of the building, the nondescript entrance was very deceiving. The yellow siding and green awning, which could stand a good power wash, didn't seem to fit on the block.

"So this is it, huh?"

"Yes, this place has the best burgers." Paul turned in his seat and caressed the back of Martina's neck, his fingers tangled in her shoulder length curls.

"Ready to go in?"

"Ready when you are."

Paul smiled as he walked around the front of the car to the passenger side. He remembered the first few times he had taken her out. She wouldn't wait for him to open the car door. Times had changed.

He extended his hand to help her out, glad for any physical contact. It surprised him when she didn't pull away as they walked toward the building.

Once inside, they strolled up to a long bar with a huge chalkboard against the wall listing its menu items. Paul ordered the chicken bacon burger meal and of course, Martina had to try something unusual. She ordered the peanut butter bacon burger.

"Maybe we should have ordered you a backup burger just in case you don't like the one you ordered," Paul said. Despite the chilly weather, he directed Martina to the outdoor eating area.

"I couldn't resist trying that combination." They found a round table on the deck overlooking the city. Since Paul wasn't sure how heated their conversation would get, he was glad the table sat away from the others and near an overhead heater.

"Man, you weren't kidding when you said the views were amazing. The scenery is almost as good as the ones you have at your place."

"I agree. The front of the building is deceiving. And wait until you try the burgers. Outstanding."

"We'll see. I'm a hamburger-ologist and right now, Teddy's Bar and Grill have the best."

"Okay. We'll see."

Once their order number was called, Paul went to the counter and brought their meal to the table.

"I can't wait for you to tell me about that burger.

I've tried other menu items, but haven't been adventurous enough to try that one."

He watched and waited as Martina bit into the burger. The erotic moans she made after the first two bites had him contemplating whether or not he should carry her off to the nearest closet and have his way with her.

"Oh. My. God. This is incredible," she cooed. "You were right. If this is any indication of the other burgers, this place is definitely the best."

Paul shook his head. "Yeah but I can't get with that combination."

"Don't knock it until you try it buddy." She held her sandwich out to him. Though he wasn't too thrilled to taste the combination, he couldn't pass up an opportunity to have his mouth where she'd just had hers.

He took a healthy bite and sat back in his seat, holding her gaze as he chewed. When she smiled at him, he couldn't help but smile.

"You're right. It is good."

Small talk flowed easily between them until they got to the subject that always had them in disagreement.

"Paul, you and your state cronies must know that if you strip the unions of their collective bargaining rights, the livelihoods of thousands of working class citizens will be impacted. Employees won't get a chance to negotiate compensation. Training opportunities will be limited, and that's just for starters." She leaned forward, lowering her voice. "The employers will have all the power. Leaving the unions with their current power is one of the main ways in which those of us who are middle class can keep moving upwardly and prosper. And if that's not enough, maybe you should remember that collective bargaining is a human right."

Though Paul didn't totally agree with her rationale, he respected her passion and the way she fought for those whose voices might not be heard. Throwing in the human rights aspect was an interesting twist.

The collective bargaining principle had been instituted to give groups like unions more bargaining power to represent employees. The notion of strength in numbers versus individual employees trying to negotiate on their own behalf had played a major role in keeping unions strong.

"Baby, we understand all of that, but you're not looking at the big picture. This bill is not just about the trades unions. This is mainly about public employees who work for the government and school systems. The governor feels that it's time we start reining in the unions to prepare them for state aid cuts, which are coming. And I agree with him. Unions were created to keep companies from exploiting workers, but now many employers are dependent on state funding…"

"Paul, you guys just want to control everything. You don't care that some human rights will be threatened," Martina argued again.

They went back and forth with their individual beliefs and concerns. Martina admitted to understanding where the Republicans were coming from and what they were trying to accomplish, but she still felt as if they were cutting the unions off at the knees. The government was weakening their bargaining power no matter how she viewed it.

After a while, both she and Paul realized they

would never agree on the subject.

"Can we just agree that there are some aspects of this situation that we will never agree on?" he asked.

"Fine, but this discussion isn't over. I'm going to continue to be an advocate for the underdog. I'm one of them."

They sat in silence until he said. "Duly noted."

*

As the sun slowly dipped behind the horizon, and the outdoor lights of the café flickered on, Martina stood nestled in Paul's embrace. They stared out at the city lights. For the most part, the space had cleared out except for them. Paul had been right about the view. It was spectacular. The whole evening had been wonderful. Even their debate regarding the collective bargaining bill hadn't put a damper on their time together.

Each passing minute with him, a little part of Martina's self-control chipped away, leaving her open to his charm. So what if they didn't always agree politically. He was such a sweetheart. Not only was he pleasing to the eye, but also one of the most thoughtful men she knew and he had the patience of Job. Even she knew that dealing with her on any level wasn't for the weak at heart.

There were moments in the past when she regretted walking away from him, but she knew it was for the best. She kept reminding herself that they wanted different things in life. But if that were the case, why was she weakening? Why was she thinking that she wanted him back? She wanted what they once had.

Paul placed a kiss against her temple. "What's going on in that gorgeous head of yours?"

She smiled up at him. Instead of sharing her thoughts, she said, "Everything was delicious, and I am stuffed."

He bent down and pecked her lips. "You're so petite. I have often wondered where you put all of the food you eat."

She laughed and then yelped when he squeezed one of her butt cheeks.

"All right, Senator. You keep touching me like that, and you're going to get something started," she said saucily. Sitting across from him all evening had been a challenge. Those sexy brown eyes of his held enough warmth to make her melt in her seat. And each time he reached out and touched her, whether a touch to her hand, or playing in her hair, the sexual tension between them amped up more.

"Ready to get out of here?" he asked grabbing hold of her hand.

"Ready when you are."

They made their way back inside and through the small, lively establishment. Martina planned to tell her cousins about the place.

"So when was the last time you were here?" Martina asked when they made it to the door.

"I brought my two nieces here over the summer. At three and five years old, I thought they would like the place since they love hamburgers and fries."

"I take it that wasn't the case."

"Not even close," he said and helped her into the car before going around to the driver's side. "I have come to understand with them it's more about the atmosphere than the food. They wanted to know where the play equipment was. When I told them this place didn't have one, they agreed that they liked

McDonald's better."

Martina laughed. Paul had told her story after story about his nieces and nephews. She could tell how much he enjoyed them.

"I wish I had a few nieces and nephews. Sounds like you guys have a good time together."

"They're great. I don't get to see my nephew who lives in L.A. as often, but when everyone is together, it's pretty wild." He headed toward Cincinnati. "Who knows, maybe you'll have a chance to be an auntie one day."

"Well, that's not going to happen since I'm an only child."

"That's not the only way to be an aunt, Martina." When she frowned at him, trying to figure out what he was talking about, he came to a stop at a traffic light and glanced at her, warmth swimming in his eyes. "You could always marry someone who has nieces and nephews."

Martina chuckled. "That's not going to happen. I'm not the marrying type."

It was Paul's turn to frown. He pulled into a gas station and parked near one of the pumps. "What do you mean you're not the marrying type? There's a type?"

"Of course, there's a type." She immediately thought of Jada, who had talked about marriage daily since she was five years old. "I'm not one of those women who has dreamed of marriage. Heck, I can't even imagine myself married. My personality is not conducive to having a husband."

Paul burst out laughing. "I have heard you say some crazy things, but this has to take the cake."

"I'm serious, Paul. I'm judgmental, stubborn,

impulsive, inflexible at times, greedy when it comes to food, and I talk back…a lot. And you know that better than anyone."

"Oh yeah, I know. But sweetheart there is so much more to you than you listed. I know for a fact that you're marriage material." He turned slightly. "Now let me give you my list."

"Paul."

"Hear me out. You have a good heart though you would have people believe otherwise. I have witnessed you pull your car over to give a homeless woman money *and* your jacket, only after she refused to let you take her to a shelter. And what about the puppy that wandered onto your work site?"

Martina smiled at that. Terry was the cutest little Shih Tzu she had ever seen.

"Not only did you rescue him, you also took care of him for two weeks until you were able to find him the perfect home. We only dated six months and I can think of many other instances. Martina, you are a loving, compassionate, fun, and exciting woman. You don't trip when a man has to work late, you love sports, you're not afraid to eat in front of a man, *and* you can throw down in the kitchen…and," his voice dipped an octave, "in the bedroom."

She stared into eyes that held so much love and desire. She didn't know what to say. Hearing him talk about her personality traits in a positive way meant a lot.

"Thank you. That's very nice of you to say."

"And it's all true."

With his hand on the back of her head, he pulled her to him, and their lips touched. She kissed back with everything in her. She knew they didn't want the same things out of a relationship, but there was one thing she was sure they both wanted and if he kept kissing her with so much passion, she would give it to him.

But there was something she needed to get straight before they could act on the sexual tension that had been jockeying between them.

Martina pulled back slightly and cupped his cheek. "Paul, I have goals I still haven't accomplished and marriage would just get in the way. And you know me. I'm okay with just hanging out, dating, and having some fun." She dropped her hand and sat back. "I'm not interested in falling in love and getting married. I already have a full life. I don't need a man to complete me."

She looked up to see him staring at her, sensing he didn't believe her little speech. Seconds ticked by before he spoke.

"Do you think you would ever allow yourself to fall in love with anyone?"

Martina swallowed and picked at some invisible lint on her jeans.

I already have, she thought, finally able to admit it to herself. But she couldn't tell him, and she recognized a loaded question when she heard one.

"I don't need marriage to prove I love someone," she finally said.

He deserved to know the truth. She wanted to tell him the truth about what she felt for him, but she couldn't. She couldn't allow herself to be vulnerable to a man. Any man.

She didn't know how her mother put her heart out there to men, knowing at some point they were going to crush it and toss it back at her. Martina couldn't.

She had witnessed her mother's heart breaks too many times to follow in those footsteps.

"I have no desire to settle down, especially since I would probably do or say something stupid and screw it up anyway," she added. "And besides all of that, most men would probably want kids. That's something else I can't picture."

Paul studied her for a minute before saying, "That's not what I asked you, Martina. I didn't ask you about marriage. I asked if you think you can ever allow yourself to fall in love."

CHAPTER TEN

Paul watched emotions flash across Martina's features, before she turned her head and stared out the passenger window. How could they move beyond this conversation, when she wouldn't share what the problem was?

Frustration rattled through him when she didn't answer.

"Baby, what are you afraid of?"

"I'm not afraid of anything," she snapped. "Why are we having this conversation? I agreed to go out to dinner with you. I didn't agree to an interrogation!"

Paul backed off. They were having a great evening. The last thing he wanted to do was ruin it with an argument. He needed to stick with his original plan. Remind and show Martina how good they once were together. Show her how good they could be together again. They were perfect for each other in every way, and he was determined to get her to see that no matter how long it took.

"I'm sorry. You're right. I shouldn't have pushed."

"And I shouldn't have yelled."

His eyebrows lifted. "Was that an apology? The almighty, always right, Martina Jenkins is apologizing for something? Well, I'll be damned."

"There you go being a smartass again." Her lips twitched as she tried holding back a smile.

Unable to resist, he leaned over and pulled her to him, ravishing her mouth. He loved her smart mouth and everything else about her. Each time their lips touched, or he held her in his arms, it became more difficult to stop at just kissing and hugging. He wanted so much more. And by the way she kissed him, he knew she wanted more as well.

They finally pulled apart, and he stepped out of the car to fill the gas tank. The night had been great, and he didn't want to drop her off at home and then just leave. But for the sake of not wanting to move too fast, he would.

Fifteen minutes later, they sat talking in his car, staring out at her house, neither wanting the evening to end.

"Are you sure you can't come in?" Martina asked and he could have sworn her voice had dipped an octave. "You can at least have a cup of coffee with me."

He was prepared to decline, but Martina caught him totally off guard when she reached over and tugged on the lapel of his jacket, forcing him closer.

"If not coffee, maybe something el..." Her last word was smothered as she covered his mouth with hers. This bold woman had the power to knock all common sense from his mind when she took the lead.

He drank in the sweetness of her kiss as blood

pounded through his veins, leaped over his heart and shot straight to his groin.

His fingers combed through her hair and stopped at the back of her head, holding her in place as their tongues tangled. The center console cut into his side, preventing him from taking what he wanted.

Okay, why was he torturing them both? They wanted this. They needed this. And who was he to turn down coffee, or anything else she had to offer?

No! His mind screamed and he broke off the kiss.

"I can't." Had that just come out of his mouth? Clearly, he was the stupidest man on earth for turning down a fascinating woman like Martina when she was offering him her body.

"I want you like a thirsty man who has just spent the last year on a deserted island without water, but I can't do this again, Martina. I want more than just your amazing body."

Her eyes narrowed, and she glared at him as if he had lost his mind. In all honesty, maybe he had, but he had to be strong and not fall under her spell again.

"Fine!" she snapped. "Your loss." She fumbled with the door handle trying to get out of the car.

"Wait. I'll walk you to the door."

"Don't bother. Just watch this *amazing* body walk away from you." She jumped out of the car and didn't look back. He half expected her to flip him the bird, but that didn't happen.

"Yep, stupidest man on the planet," he murmured, but he had to take a stand with her. Otherwise, they would end up where they left off. Great sex. No commitment.

*

Martina stormed into the house and slammed the

door, tossing her keys onto a nearby table.

"Ugh!" She threw up her arms. How the hell could he kiss her like that and then let her go? Adrenaline pumped through her veins like a gushing oil well. She inhaled and then exhaled slowly trying to regain control. He had her so worked up, that she had been tempted to climb into his lap inside the car. But then he brought everything to a halt.

Damn him for thinking too much!

She snatched off her jacket and threw it across the room. When the garment missed the sofa and landed on the floor, her frustration skyrocketed. Heat flooded her body as she thought about that kiss and her sex clenched with need.

"Oh that man!" she screamed.

Still feeling hot and bothered, Martina yanked off her shirt, leaving her in a tank top. She kicked off her shoes and stomped around the living room fanning herself.

She had given Paul an open invitation and the man turned her down. That was a first. She always got what she wanted with him…until now.

Martina dropped down on the sofa and pounded the cushions. Why couldn't he understand that she didn't do serious relationships? She had to protect herself. She had to protect her heart. Letting Paul get too close again would be a bad idea. A very bad idea.

You can lie to us, but don't keep lying to yourself. Peyton's words infiltrated Martina's thoughts.

"No. No. No!" She shook her head, the back of her hair rubbing against the sofa. "I am not still in love with Paul. I can't be." But she knew the truth. She had never stopped loving him.

Maybe it's good he left.

The last thing she needed was to get addicted to him all over again. Back then, she could barely go a minute without thinking about him or wanting to be anywhere he was, but now she was back in control.

"Yeah, it's good he brought a halt to our make-out session," she said out loud. But then she moaned and sagged deeper into the sofa. "Who am I kidding?"

The doorbell rang.

Martina froze.

When seconds ticked by and the bell didn't ring again, she assumed she was hearing things. But then someone pounded on the front door.

A smile tugged at her lips, and she leaped up, hurrying across the room. The sexual desire stampeding through her body only moments ago returned with a vengeance when she swung the door open and found Paul standing there.

"Don't say a word," he growled and stepped into the house, kicking the door closed. They didn't get beyond the foyer before his mouth swooped down over hers. His large hands palmed her ass, pulling her against his erection and Martina whimpered as he ground against her.

With a hand on her waist, he backed her to the wall, groping at the bottom of her tank top before lifting it over her head and tossing it to the floor. They clawed at each other's clothes, panting as his jacket, shirt and her jeans flew around the small space like leaves blowing in a storm.

Left in their underwear, they lunged back into each other's arms, his large hands all over her body. Pulse beating eagerly, Martina held on as his tongue hungrily explored the inner recesses of her mouth. His kiss frantic, yet thorough and she gave as good as she got, happy to be back in his arms again.

A moan filled the silence of the house and Martina didn't know if it had come from her or him. She didn't care. All she knew was that she wasn't letting him out of the house until she reminded him of how good they were together.

His breath was warm against her body as he trailed heated kisses along her jaw line and kept moving south.

"God, you smell delicious," he nibbled against her neck. His hands skimmed down her body, stopping at her breasts. "Mmm, and you feel even better."

Martina inhaled when his thumbs caressed her sensitive nipples. Her knees went weak as desire nicked every nerve ending within her. She couldn't ever remember wanting anyone as bad as she wanted him right then and there.

"I want you," he said hoarsely as if reading her mind. "But not here."

He bent down. Quickly rummaging through his pant pockets, he found his wallet and removed a condom. Before Martina could form her next thought, Paul lifted her as if she weighed nothing and carried her to the bedroom. When he set her on her feet, her gaze dropped to the bulge barely contained behind his black boxer briefs. She was already eager to get up close and personal, but seeing the outline of his thick package, begging to be free, sent a rush of excitement straight to her core.

Paul stood frozen, the foil packet between his fingers. Heat scorched her skin as his gaze did a slow drag down her body, taking in her lavender, matching bra and panty set. She didn't spend much money on clothes, but Martina did invest well in pretty underwear. And with the hunger radiating in his eyes, she was glad she had.

Paul wasn't the only one getting an eye full. There hadn't been much light in the hallway, but now Martina took in his wide shoulders that tapered down to a narrow waist. His washboard abs made her itch to run her hands up and down his eight pack. And were his biceps even bigger than they once were? Martina had seen his buffed body plenty of times, but tonight…

"Damn, you're even more beautiful than I remember." The roughness of his voice held so much emotion as he moved toward her.

"And you're even *hotter* than I remember."

Paul grinned and tossed the foil packet onto the side table. He placed his hands on her hips. "I have missed you."

Martina's heart thundered and her hands glided up his smooth, bare chest. She loved the way his muscles rippled beneath her touch. His closeness reminded her of what she'd been missing. Him. All of him.

"I've missed you too." She draped her arms around his neck and gently pulled on the back of his head, bringing his mouth closer. Martina gave herself freely to the passion of their kiss. She already knew one time with him wouldn't be enough. He had weakened her resolve to keep distance between them.

"I want to see all of you." He unhooked the clasp of her bra with expert fingers and eased the straps down her arms, tossing the material aside. Her skimpy panties quickly followed.

"My turn." She glided her hands down the side of his taut body until she reached the band of his boxer briefs. An involuntary groan rumbled in her throat as she pushed them down his thick legs, his shaft standing at attention.

Paul kicked the briefs off, and Martina bit down on her bottom lip to keep from groaning again at his exquisite body. Unable to resist, her hand enclosed around his length and she smiled when he heaved a ragged breath.

"Mmm, you feel good." Her hand slid up and down his shaft, squeezing and gently tugging, loving the way he grew within her grasp.

Paul cursed under his breath and grabbed hold of her wrist, halting her actions.

"Okay, okay. If you keep touching me like that, this will be over before we start." He backed her up, easing her onto the queen size bed and climbed on next to her.

Part of Martina wanted to hurry this seduction scene along, but the other part of her wanted to go slow and get reacquainted with each other's body.

"I plan to savor every minute of my time with you," Paul said. His low baritone voice sent a shiver up Martina's spine as he stroked and teased one of her nipples. A deep guttural moan escaped from the back of her throat, and her eyes drifted closed. She delighted in his touch. This is what her body needed, what her body craved.

She shuddered when his mouth took the place of his fingers. He pulled a pert nipple between his teeth, gently tugging before swirling his tongue around the hardened bud. She squeezed her thighs together, wiggling against him as her sex pulsated with need.

"Paul," she whined, but he continued the sweet torture. One of his hands seared a path down the center of her body and didn't stop until he reached the opening between her thighs.

Body heat spiking, Martina whimpered, grabbing a handful of the sheet in her fist. His finger, like a heat-seeking missile, found her throbbing sex and he glided the first digit inside of her and then added a second. Between the sweet torment that his mouth was doing on her nipple and the exploration of his fingers, Martina knew she couldn't hold on much longer.

Her hips moved in rhythm with his fingers while he slid in and out, stroking, teasing, and bringing her body alive. "Paul," she gasped, unable to form a sentence. Her heart beat triple time. Passion brewed to explosive proportions and her control teetered on the edge. Martina hadn't felt this aroused since the last time she was with him and…

Paul lifted his head, her nipple popping from his mouth. He increased the speed of his fingers, pressing deeper and harder.

"Paul!" Her head thrashed against the mound of pillows. "I...I…"

"Come for me baby."

As soon as he spoke the words, an orgasm gripped her and she bucked wildly against his hand. She screamed a release as her body jerked and thrashed uncontrollably.

Oh my God. She panted, clutching his arms, her fingernails digging into his skin while she gasped for air. *Oh my God.*

*

Waves of ecstasy throbbed through Paul as he watched Martina crumble to pieces. He quickly grabbed the foil packet on the side table and ripped it open with his teeth, yearning to be inside of her.

How many times had he dreamed of being with her again?

He eased between her legs and nudged her thighs further apart, kissing her soft lips.

"That was…we…"

"We're just getting started, baby," Paul crooned.

Martina's sizzling orgasm only fueled the flames burning within him. Making love to her always gave him a chance to see her gentler side, where she lowered her guards and gave into passion.

Paul so wanted to take this slow, but her enticing body and womanly curves only made him harder. He slid into her sweet heat and his heart slammed against his chest. It was as if he had finally made it home. Her inner muscles wrapped around him like a snug fitting glove.

Having her again this way, stirred another emotion within him – longing. He wanted her back in his life permanently, and he intended to have her.

She's mine. She's mine.

The words looped in his mind. He increased his pace, pumping harder, faster, going deeper, encouraged by the erotic sounds emanating from deep within her. Memories of their times together flooded back. Martina is what he wanted, what he needed in his life.

Paul lifted her hip off the bed and slid in deeper. His thrust grew frantic, and he was like an out-of-control freight train ramping up speed, faster and faster. Martina matched him stroke for stroke, her muscles contracting around his shaft.

"Mar…tina!" he growled between gritted teeth when she wrapped her legs around his waist and squeezed her thighs tight. Paul cursed under his breath. She was sucking his control right out of him while he struggled to hold on.

"P…Paul," she stuttered, her fingers digging into his thighs.

"Come with me baby." Paul pumped faster.

"Paul!" Martina screamed her release and Paul was right behind her, holding her tightly. His release hit him fast and hard as he roared her name, his world spinning out of control.

He collapsed on top of her, unable to think, barely able to breathe. Martina wrapped her arms around him, breathing hard against his neck.

Finally able to move, Paul rolled to his side, taking Martina with him. Sated, he held her in his arms, placing a kiss on her sweat-slicked forehead. Heavy panting filled the quietness of the room.

Minutes ticked by before Martina eventually broke the silence saying, "Ready for round two?"

Paul chuckled and kissed her again. "Definitely, but give me a minute."

CHAPTER ELEVEN

Paul snuggled his face deeper into the scented pillow that he held onto like a lifeline, not ready to regain full consciousness. He had no idea what time it was, and he didn't care. All he wanted to do was freeze time and stay just as he was, wrapped in the warmth of the soft blanket.

The smell of food permeated the air and tickled his nostrils. His head popped up, and he struggled to open his eyes and clear the fog of sleep from his mind. He lived alone. So the smell of food, when he wasn't the one cooking was a little unnerving.

Turning in bed, his gaze took in the unfamiliar room. Bold abstract art graced the light gray walls with white crown molding bringing a sophisticated look to the space. The dark furniture wasn't overly big, but neither was the room. Everything was neat, orderly. And then he heard someone whistling a soft melody in the distance.

Martina.

Memories of the night before bombarded him, and

he dropped back onto the pillow, smiling as he recalled the wild night.

The woman damn near killed him.

She had more energy, and passion than anyone he knew. He was still finding it hard to believe they had hooked back up. And in a big way. But then something else dawned on him. They were back where they left off. Smoking hot sex. No commitment.

Frustration churned through his body. The night before he'd been blinded by her boldness and her fine tail, but this morning, he needed to make sure his head was on straight. No way could he go back to what they once had when he wanted every stubborn inch of her, mind and body. He appreciated a good challenge, but if he couldn't get her to give them another try and not just sex, then he was going to have to find a way to move on and not look back.

"Don't think too hard. You might hurt yourself." The sultry voice came from the doorway. He lifted up on his elbows and took in her appearance.

All the self-talk from moments ago flew right out the window.

Her lovely face, free of makeup, held a sexy smile that was like a punch in the gut. She seemed so sweet and harmless, but he knew better. The woman was a detriment to his peace of mind and one look at her had him aching with need to be inside of her again.

Still unable to speak, his gaze soaked her up. She wore his dress shirt, with only the two middle buttons fastened, and her bare legs appeared longer than usual. His erection grew harder if that were possible, and his eyes dropped lower to her bare feet accented with purple painted toenails.

To say she looked sexy would be an understatement.

Yep, she was definitely trying to kill him.

He dropped back onto the pillow and closed his eyes, covering them with his forearm.

Her soft steps against the carpeted floor met his ears as they drew closer, and then her side of the bed dipped.

"So, I don't get a good morning, which means you were overthinking last night."

All he could do was grunt.

"It also means you're probably kicking yourself for falling under my spell…again."

He chuckled, unable to stop himself.

"Arrogant much?" he mumbled. He didn't have to remove his arm from his eyes to know she had a Cheshire cat grin spread across her gorgeous face.

"Instead of *talking*, like I'm sure you think we should do, how about breakfast? I made some of your favorites. Mushroom and tomato omelet, turkey sausage, and a side of mouth-watering, blueberry pancakes. And if that doesn't temp you, there is a cup of strong, black coffee with your name on it."

"Though I could eat a horse right about now, you're the only thing tempting me." Paul turned, pulling her close. With his hands caressing her body, he proved what he had assumed. She wasn't wearing anything under his shirt.

"Now you're talking." She stripped off the shirt, tossing it to the floor. "But this time I'm on top."

∗

"I thought we were spending the rest of the day at your place, where are you going?" Martina asked when she realized he wasn't driving toward his Mt.

Adams home.

"I need to pick up Charlie," Paul said of his collie mix. "My sister, Myra, kept him while I was out of town."

Martina said nothing. He had talked about his two sisters and their families on numerous occasions. If she remembered correctly, Myra was the lawyer who had three children. His other sister, Kacey, was a doctor and married with one child.

Martina hadn't met either of them. Not because he didn't want her to, but because she didn't want to. The subject was a part of many of their disagreements. Like her, family was important to him. Her hesitance came by way of fear that it would look as if they were a couple back then. She'd done everything she could to keep their relationship casual until he'd messed everything up.

Martina had forgotten about Charlie. Paul mentioned the night before that he had to pick up the dog once he dropped her off at home. Thanks to their rendezvous, that didn't happen.

He pulled into the long driveway of a large, two-story brick home and cut the engine.

He exited the vehicle and walked around the front of the car to the passenger side.

Martina just stared at him when he opened the door and extended his hand.

"What? I'm not going in. It shouldn't take that long. I can wait out here."

"Martina I'm not leaving you out here. You're right, it probably won't take long, but I'm not leaving you in the car. Let's go."

She glanced from his face to his hand and back up again. Spending the entire day lounging around with him, watching college football in between lovemaking sessions had been perfect.

"Paul—"

"I know you didn't want to meet my family when we were dating, but we're friends. Or at least I'd like to think we are. You have nothing to worry about. You going in with me, possibly meeting my sister means nothing. So can you stop being difficult and come with me? It's too cold out here to be arguing. Besides, the kids love the dog and are never ready for him to leave. And my sister will try to insist that I stay for dinner. By having you with me, that'll help me get outta there quicker."

After their talk over breakfast, he had agreed that they could take their reunion slow. Of course, she insisted they should just hang out and get reacquainted, but he told her that he already knew her. As before, he wanted more than she was willing to give. She planned to show him that they were good together. They didn't have to mess up the natural flow of things with discussions of marriage and kids.

"Fine," she finally said and swiped his hand away as she climbed out of the car unassisted. "While you're laying a guilt trip on me, you could've gone in, gotten Charlie, and we could be on our way."

"Yeah, but then I wouldn't have had this little verbal sparring with you. It's great practice for when I have to argue a point during some of my committee meetings." The humor in his voice and the kiss he planted on top of her head did nothing to calm her nerves.

She talked a tough game, but the inside of her stomach twisted into knots. They agreed to take their relationship slow. Meeting his family felt too personal...too scary.

Martina heard Charlie bark the moment Paul rang the doorbell and she mentally braced herself for whatever came next. She wiped her sweaty palms down the sides of her slacks. Her heart pounded double time. Not much made her nervous, but meeting a member of Paul's family for the first time was doing just that.

"Sit." A woman's command came from the other side of the door. After a few minutes, all Martina heard was whimpering.

"Hey, I thought you were pick—" his sister, Myra, started but stopped when she saw Martina standing next to Paul. She readjusted the baby that was on her hip, and before she could stop him, Charlie lunged at Paul.

"Hey buddy." Paul greeted his dog who was standing on its hind legs.

Martina didn't miss the way Myra's brows rose in question, her gaze bouncing from Paul to her. Tall and slender with a cute bob hairstyle, she was even prettier than the pictures Paul had around his old apartment.

"Uncle Paul!" An adorable little girl with two long ponytails hanging from each side of her head screamed as she charged toward the door. Paul caught the child with his free arm and lifted her.

"Okay, okay, I guess you guys are glad to see me."

Martina watched in amusement as he gave his niece a noisy kiss while ruffling Charlie's fur. Her heart split open just a little at the sight of him loving on the girl with such affection. Martina knew he would be a loving father someday.

As if just noticing her, Charlie barked his greeting.

He hurried over to her and leaped up, putting him near her height. Marina stumbled back, trying to stay upright.

"Down!" Paul ordered, his free hand on her back, holding her steady. Charlie went back to all fours before sitting, his tail thumping wildly. "You okay?" Paul asked, concern on his face.

"I'm fine." Martina bent and hugged Charlie. She turned her head in time for his doggy kiss to land on her neck instead of her face. "Hey, sweet boy. Long time no see." She and Charlie use to spend a lot of time together, especially when Paul traveled and she dog sat.

Another, smaller, child barreled towards them. She wrapped her arms around Paul's legs, begging to be picked up.

"Peanut, get a hold of your dog, and you guys come in," Myra said.

Martina's lips twitched at the nickname. Paul glared, daring her to say something smart.

He grabbed hold of Charlie's collar. "All right, boy. Let's give Martina some space."

His sister opened the door wider and stepped aside. With a hand at the small of her back, Paul ushered Martina inside.

"Hey sis, this is a friend of mine, Martina Jenkins. Martina this is my sister, Myra."

"It's a pleasure to meet you, Martina."

"You too."

"Well you two make yourself comfortable. I'm preparing dinner and need to get back in there and check on the food. Here," Myra handed Paul the baby, "hold him for a second or you can put him in his chair, in the family room. Oh, and girls, don't ask

Ms. Martina too many questions."

"Hey lil man," Paul cooed at the baby who practically had his whole hand in his little mouth, drool dripping down his chin. He was also staring at Martina.

"Hi there." She tugged on the baby's bare feet, extracting a grin from him.

"This here is Collin. He just turned ten months, and it looks as if he's as enthralled by you as I am."

"Uncle Paul, what's entall mean?" the tallest of the girls asked, butchering the word.

"What's your name?" the smallest girl asked Martina before Paul could respond to her sister.

"And it begins," Paul grumbled.

Martina laughed and bent slightly to the little girl. "My name is MJ. What's your name?"

"Her name is Aliyah, and my name is Ann-Marie. I have the same name as Daddy's mommy," the oldest girl said.

"That's awesome, Ann-Marie. You and Aliyah have pretty names."

They each grabbed ahold of her hands, both talking at the same time as they pulled her into the family room. Martina glanced over her shoulder at Paul, who shrugged and mouthed *sorry*.

*

Forty-five minutes later, Paul stood in the doorway of his sister's family room watching Martina interact with his nieces. She laughed at their antics and listened attentively while the youngest tried to tell her something about the movie they were watching on TV.

This was the Martina that people rarely had a chance to see, the sweet, patient, compassionate woman who loved children.

"How old are you?" Paul heard Aliyah ask Martina.

"I'm thirty-one."

Both girl's eyes grew big.

"Whoa," Aliyah said.

"Wait. Is that old?" Ann-Marie asked, her brows scrunched in confusion.

Martina laughed and pinched Ann-Marie's cheek. "Yes, that's old. Well, older than you."

"You've been holding out on us, Peanut. She's cute."

That she is, Paul thought, ignoring the nickname that he hated. His gaze took in Martina. Actually, cute wasn't a strong enough word to describe her. In fact, she was the most beautiful woman he'd ever laid eyes on.

"I take it that you've known her awhile. Charlie hasn't left her side since you two arrived. So how long have you guys been dating and why am I just meeting her?" she whispered, nudging him in the arm.

As for Charlie, he and Martina had always got along well. There were even times when Charlie seemed to favor her over him.

"I kept her to myself because I didn't want you to scare her away," he joked. "But seriously, right now we're just … hanging out. We dated over a year ago for a while, but things didn't work out." Now wasn't the time, if ever, to give her all the details of his and Martina's history.

"Well, I like her. Anyone who can sit through Aliyah's explanation of *Despicable Me* and seem interested in the movie is alright in my book." She moved farther into the room and clapped her hands.

"All right you munchkins. I want you two to go into that bedroom and get all of those toys off the floor."

"But Mom, MJ might be gone by then," Ann-Marie argued.

"That's Ms. MJ to you, young lady. And if you and your sister would have picked up that room when I first told you to, it would have already been done. Then you wouldn't have to stop interrogating Ms. MJ. Now go!"

"What's interogay mean?" Ann-Marie questioned.

Paul shook his head and chuckled when his sister rolled her eyes. Ann-Marie was like a little sponge soaking up every bit of knowledge she could, which meant asking fifty-million questions every day.

"Come on. I'll explain it to you while we clean up." She hustled the girls to the door. "Are you guys able to stay for dinner?" Myra asked.

Paul glanced at Martina who was giving Charlie her full attention, talking to him while scratching behind his ears. Paul still couldn't believe she had agreed to come into the house without more of a fuss. He probably shouldn't have made such a big deal about coming in with him, but it was. He wanted her in his life, and that meant meeting his family. He knew he couldn't woo her or pull her into his life the traditional way. Heck, there was nothing traditional about Martina. But Paul was determined to get to the bottom of her commitment phobia if it was the last thing he did.

"Sis, I think we're going to head out."

Martina seemed to have a good time with his family, but he didn't want to push his luck. Besides, he had big, *adult*, plans for her when he got her to his house.

*

Martina nestled deeper into her wool coat and relaxed against the soft leather seats in Paul's car, staring out of the passenger window as the city buzzed by. The October chill reminded her that summer was over, and winter lurked just around the corner.

Her mind drifted back to Paul's sister and her family. Prior to them leaving, Myra's husband had arrived home, and they all stood around talking sports. Martina felt as if she had known the couple forever. They were so down to earth considering they were both lawyers.

Now as she sat next to Paul, she had to admit that she had probably over thought the idea of meeting his family. The visit wasn't uncomfortable at all. Maybe letting the guard around her heart down a little would be okay.

A dose of what ifs popped into her head. What if she allowed Paul to get a little closer? What if she let him put a title on whatever was currently happening between them? And what if she allowed him to meet her grandparents?

Martina startled when Charlie whimpered. She had been talking to him from the front seat for the first few minutes of their drive. Now she'd been in her own little world while he was stuck in the back seat inside his crate, which he hated, but Paul insisted on.

"What are you thinking about?" Paul asked, squeezing her thigh.

She hesitated before speaking but covered his hand with hers.

"Your family. Us. My family." She kept her gaze down, playing with his long, tapered fingers. She didn't know whether or not to go into details about the thoughts playing around in her mind. Paul wanted forever. After their talk that morning about picking up where they had left off a year ago, she was pretty sure that wouldn't change. Like before, he claimed he could handle a casual relationship, but she wasn't so sure he could. Heck, she wasn't so sure she could.

"So what were you thinking about all of us?" he prompted.

"I was thinking about how nice it was meeting your family. Myra and her husband seems cool. And the kids are great."

"But ... because it sounds like there's a but coming."

"No but, just an observation. Thanks for insisting I meet them. I had a good time."

"It seems like something else is on your mind. You're a little distracted. *Is* there something else?"

"Yes…no," she stammered, frustrating herself. "I mean…what do you think about attending Sunday brunch with me, tomorrow at my grandparent's house?"

Oh, crap! What the heck?

The surprised look on his face matched the shock that slammed inside her chest. She could only imagine what the expression on her face looked like.

She wasn't sure what she had planned to say to him, but she was pretty sure it wasn't that.

A stunned silence filled the car. He was probably waiting for her to say - *oops, I didn't mean to say that.* And her mind screamed - *tell him that's not what you meant!*

The silence grew, sitting between them like a two-ton boulder, unable to be moved with no room to go around it.

What was I thinking? I can't take him to Sunday brunch.

Every Sunday, her grandmother spearheaded a huge meal where the whole family gathered to eat, watch sports, play games, and talk crazy to each other. Though the house was always full and lively on Sundays, the gathering was intimate…personal. The last thing Martina needed was for her family to think she and Paul were a serious couple. Peyton and the girls would eat this up, and there would be no end to the teasing.

But how was she going to get out of this?

"I'd love to go to Sunday brunch with you tomorrow." Paul interrupted her musings. "Just let me know what time."

Oh, that's just great.

CHAPTER TWELVE

The next day, Paul steered his Lexus toward the Jenkins's estate, stealing an occasional glance at Martina as she sat wringing her hands together. He couldn't remember ever seeing her so worked up, but he was pretty sure she had never taken a man to her grandparents' home. He'd bet the balance in his trust fund on it.

Martina stayed the night with him. She had been antsy from the moment she extended the invitation to the famous Jenkins family brunch. Even when he took her home, a little over an hour ago, to change clothes, she wasn't herself. Walking around aimlessly, mumbling to herself, she was barely able to look him in the eyes, and she'd been quiet. Too quiet.

The night before, Paul sensed the invite caught her off guard as much as it had surprised him. For a moment, he thought about letting her off the hook and not going, but where was the fun in that? It was way past time Martina faced her fear of commitment, and he was just the man to help her along.

"Martina, relax." He reached for her hand and squeezed. "Everything is going to be fine."

She shook her head. "I don't know Paul. This might be a bad idea. Being around my family can be a little overwhelming at times. You don't know what you're in for."

"Your family cannot be worse than mine. I doubt we'll be subjected to hearing someone like my father drone on and on about politics or hear about someone's new winter wardrobe, which would be my mother's topic of conversation."

"Don't be too sure about that. Jada, Ms. Fashionista, will be there and I guarantee she will bore us with a story about her latest designer outfit or those stupid red bottom shoes. Like anyone of us cares about that crap."

Paul laughed, glad to have his baby back to normal. As long as she was giving him a hard time, or making him laugh with stories about the life around her, that was a good sign.

"Oh and don't get me started on CJ."

"That's Christina, the artist, right? The one married to the thug lawyer?"

Martina grinned. "Yep, that's the one, but she and Luke aren't married yet. I'm sure it's only a matter of time though. But anyway, she'll be floating around the house like all is well with the world. Actually, she and her mother, my aunt Violet, mentally live in a different world. They're into harmony with nature and expressing one's self artistically. I also think they're trying to bring back the 60s, the hippie days, when it comes to their clothes."

Paul laughed again.

"And since I'm warning you about them, might as

well add Toni and Peyton to the mix. Toni will be gushing over her husband Craig and carrying little Craig around on her hip as if he can't walk. And you met Peyton. She's probably the only one of us who has good sense ... though lately, I think she's been a little depressed." Martina shrugged. "But who knows since she usually keeps everything to herself."

Paul listened, learning more about Martina's family in the forty-minute drive, than all the six months they had dated. He smiled to himself. This is what he had been waiting a long time for. Martina to let her guard down.

Paul pulled into her grandparents' circular drive, the huge home standing out in comparison to the other houses on the block. He followed Martina's direction and drove along another driveway that took them toward the back of the house in search of a parking spot.

Seconds later when they approached the back door, it swung open, barely missing Martina. Two men walked out, one Paul recognized.

"Hey, what's up, MJ?" said the man who Paul didn't recognize. His wide-eyed surprise quickly turned to amusement when a mischievous grinned spread across his face. Maybe Martina had reason to be nervous about bringing a man to Sunday brunch. If she gave her family as much grief as she gave him sometimes, they probably couldn't wait to needle her.

"Hey," Martina said, her voice shaking with a twinge of nervousness. Paul fought back the laugh that threatened to erupt.

Since it didn't seem like she was going to do introductions, he introduced himself.

"Hey fellas, I'm Paul Kendricks."

"What's up, man? I'm Luke."

"I'm Zack."

They all shook hands.

"I thought I recognized you, Senator Kendricks," Zack said. "Glad you could join us."

"It's my pleasure. And congrats on your retirement, Zack. You had an impressive football career with Cincinnati," Paul said.

"Thanks."

Zack, Jada's husband, was one of the best running backs in NFL's history and had retired a few months earlier. Now Zack stayed close to the game as a guest commentator for ESPN.

"Sooo," Luke started, "what's going on he—"

"And on that note, move it so we can get by." Martina elbowed her way pass the guys causing them to erupt in laughter.

"Oh, so it's like that?" Luke cracked. To Paul, he said, "We'll catch you later and give you the scoop on her."

Paul laughed. "I look forward to it."

"Don't encourage them, Paul," Martina grumbled and guided him into the house. They stood at the edge of a long hallway, and one couldn't miss the excited voices coming from every direction. Martina stiffened next to him, her nervousness returning despite the first introductions going well.

He placed his arm around her shoulders. "You okay?"

"No, but let's get this over with," she mumbled. He chuckled and followed her farther into the house. Luckily he wasn't easily offended. Her attitude would have sent another man fleeing out the door, but Paul wasn't bothered by her behavior. Being in politics had prepared him for anything, even Martina and her family.

As they made their way through the home, Martina introduced him to family members they bumped into along the way. They didn't stop moving until they stood in the doorway that led to the kitchen. He assumed, the women busy working, chatting, and laughing were the cousins she often mentioned.

At first, no one noticed them until Peyton glanced up. All heads turned in their direction. Silence settled over the room and all activity stopped.

For a moment, he thought he would have to introduce himself, but then Martina spoke.

"Well don't just stand there, say something," she said to the group before turning to him. "Just in case you haven't figured it out, the chatterboxes in here who have suddenly gone mute, are my cousins. And the cute short lady with the warm smile is my gramma, Katherine Jenkins."

Her grandmother stepped forward. "Well, you must be *the Senator*. Welcome to our home." Instead of accepting his hand in a handshake, she opened her arms to him.

Paul liked her immediately. Her warm hug was solid and real. Something he hadn't received from his mother in a long time.

"Well, Senator, I've heard a lot about you," Katherine said when she stepped back.

Paul's brows rose as he glanced at Martina, her gaze everywhere but on him.

He returned his attention to her grandmother. "Please call me, Paul, and hopefully, what you've heard wasn't all bad."

She laughed and squeezed his arm. "Not *all* bad.

Make yourself comfortable. We'll have the food ready shortly."

With that, she walked out of the kitchen, leaving him with Martina and her cousins, who merely stared, mouths hanging open.

"Come on, I'll show you where the guys are," Martina said, trying to push him out of the kitchen.

"Not so fast!" A voice came from behind them. "Don't even *think* about taking that man out of here before we officially meet him."

Paul turned to find the shortest of the four women standing with her hands on her hips. Not a hair was out of place. Her makeup looked professionally done, and the bling she wore in her ears and around her neck definitely screamed fashionista.

"You must be Jada," he extended his hand.

She beamed and shook his hand. "You've heard of me? See me before you leave today and I'll make sure I tell you the truth about me because I'm sure whatever she's told you," she nodded toward Martina, "was an exaggeration."

"And I don't even want to know what she told you about me. I'm CJ. Nice to finally meet you, Senator." She shook his hand and turned to Peyton. "And I think you know my sister."

"Yes. Good seeing you again, Peyton." He turned to the last person who approached. "That means you must be Toni."

"That would be me, Senator."

"Please call me Paul."

"What? Your name is Paul, not Satan's Spa—"

"I see we're right on time to save you," came a deep voice from the doorway. "Craig Logan. Nice to meet you, Paul."

"Same to you." Paul remembered that Craig was Toni's husband.

"I'm sure my wife wasn't about to say what I *think* she was about to say before Craig stopped her." Zack wrapped his arm around Jada's shoulder and placed a kiss against her temple. "Were you?"

"Of course not, baby," she said sweetly and then winked at Paul.

Paul couldn't help but laugh.

So these are the Jenkins girls. They were even livelier than he imagined.

"Come on, man. Let's get you out of here before they start asking you a million questions," Craig said to him after placing a quick kiss on his wife's lips.

"Yeah, it could get ugly," Zack added as they escorted him out of the kitchen, taking him to meet the "cool" cousins according to him.

Paul looked forward to meeting other family members. He had a feeling the afternoon was going to be both informative and entertaining.

He grabbed hold of Martina and pulled her close, placing a kiss on her cheek. "I'll see you a little later."

*

Martina groaned as her cousins talked and teased nonstop. She knew it was going to be bad, but they were taking teasing to a completely new level. Surely she wasn't this bad when they brought their significant others around.

Significant other.

Is that what Paul was to her now? If so, she wasn't sure how she felt about that. Yes, he was the sweetest man she'd ever met and yes he held a special spot in her heart. But....

"MJ and Paul sitting in a tree, K-I-S-S-I-N-G,"

Toni sang.

Bringing him to the brunch was a mistake. A big mistake.

"First comes love, then comes marriage," Christina added.

"Then comes baby in a ba—"

"Finish that sentence and I will cut you!" Martina threatened Jada with the butter knife in her hand.

"Ahh, payback is a bitch isn't it?" Jada teased.

"Watch your mouth young lady," their grandmother said when she strolled into the kitchen, tightening the belt of her apron. "And Martina, what did I tell you about threatening your cousins with knives?"

Everyone laughed except Martina. "They started it," she mumbled and continued spreading butter on the tops of the dinner rolls. She never thought that her teasing over the years would all come back to haunt her.

This is going to be a long day.

*

Two weeks later, Martina drove through Indian Hill, heading back to her grandparents' home for Sunday brunch. She had missed the week before and hadn't attended since the Sunday she brought Paul to meet the family. Introductions had gone well, and the family had treated him as if they had known him for years.

Martina pulled into her grandparents' driveway, found a parking space, and shut off the engine. Instead of heading into the house, she sat staring straight ahead. Anxiousness that built inside of her over the last few days regarding Paul, took up residence in her body. Romantic relationships weren't her thing.

"What am I going to do?" she murmured, resting her forehead on the steering wheel. She was crazy about Paul but had been avoiding him for the last two weeks, fearing things between them were developing too fast. It helped that he spent some of that time out of town, but he was back and blowing up her cell phone. Surprisingly he hadn't shown up at her house yet.

Martina startled at the knock on her truck window.

"Why are you sitting out here in the cold?" Peyton asked when Martina climbed out of her truck.

"Thinking."

Peyton shook her head. "I get nervous when you start thinking," she cracked.

Martina smiled for the first time that day. "Whatever." She bumped Peyton with her shoulder. "Considering how busy things have been at work, you should be glad you have me there to help you think."

Peyton groaned. "Let's not talk work today. Tomorrow will be here soon enough, and we'll have to put our heads together and decide how we want to handle the St. Claire job."

Martina quivered. She wasn't looking forward to that job. It wouldn't be so bad if the owner of the company weren't such a knucklehead.

"You're right, let's not talk work. I have enough on my mind."

"Would your heavy thinking have anything to do with the handsome Senator?"

"Yes."

"Want to talk about it?"

"Nope," Martina said.

Peyton slowed her steps and stole a glance at Martina. After a short hesitation, she said, "All righty then."

Martina opened the back door to the house glad Peyton didn't push for more information. Martina really had nothing to complain about as it related to Paul. He was a kind, giving, and loving man. She was the one with the issues and had no clue on how to get over them.

Hours later, after everyone had eaten and most of the family had left, Martina helped with the kitchen clean up. She couldn't wait to go home and the family was probably ready for her to leave. Martina had been snapping at everyone about every little thing from the moment she walked through the back door. And reason being – *Paul.* At some point, maybe she would have to talk to Peyton. She needed talk to someone about how to handle her feelings for Paul.

"Hey, what time are you leaving?" Carolyn, Martina's mother, asked when she strolled into the kitchen and set two empty bowls on the counter near the sink. "I want to know if you can give me a ride home."

Martina placed the bowls into the soapy dishwater. She and her mother had done a good job of staying clear of each other all afternoon. Martina had hoped she would be able to get out of there before her mother cornered her. Granted that wasn't the best attitude to have about her mother. But the last thing Martina needed was to spend a forty-five-minute drive with the two of them arguing.

They'd had a huge argument earlier regarding the other Sunday Paul attended the brunch. Martina didn't like the way her mother tried sharing stories about Martina's youth like Carolyn had been around during that time. Raised by her grandparents, for the most part, if anyone was going to share stories about her, it should be them. Not Carolyn.

"Where's your car?" Martina continued washing dishes. "I heard you got a new one."

Her mother's frustrated sigh filled the suddenly quiet kitchen. Martina didn't have to look back to know that everyone had probably stopped what they were doing to listen in.

"Daniel has it. He needed to take off early and I wasn't ready to leave. Can you give me a ride or not? I'm sick of going through this every time I ask anything of you. I'm your mother. You shouldn't have a problem dropping me off at home. I live less than a mile from you."

Martina remained silent. The thought of being stuck in a car with Carolyn for any amount of time didn't appeal to her.

"Besides," her mother continued, "you can pick up your drill while you're there. Daniel finished putting together the book shelf."

Martina thought about the drill that she had reluctantly loaned them the weekend before. Everyone knew how protective she was of her tools, and the only reason she had given in was because Carolyn had asked in front of Martina's grandmother.

"You and *Daniel* need a better system to deal with your transportation issues."

"Would it kill you to be a little nicer to Daniel?" her mother asked. "What the heck is your problem? Actually, I should be asking, what's your problem *today*, Martina? You have given me and Daniel the evil eye from the moment we arrived. He's a wonderful man. You would know that if you took the time to get to know him."

"She's right, MJ. Daniel is a nice guy." Christina moved closer to Carolyn and looped her arm around her shoulders. "Auntie, you did a stupendous job picking this one. He's caliente!" She shook out her hand as if being burned.

Martina rolled her eyes.

"Oh and it hasn't gone unnoticed," Christina continued, "his proclivity to take care of you is endearing, catering to your every need. You might have found a real vanquisher this time."

"Oh give me a break," Martina murmured, watching as her mother laughed and joked with Christina. How could they make light of the fact that her mother changed men every other month?

"How do you expect me to act?" Martina dried her hands and moved closer. "He's the third guy you have brought around us in the last six months. When are you going to grow up and figure out how to hold onto one man, at least for more than a few months? And you wonder why I don't want to be anything like you."

Hurt radiated in her mother's eyes and for a minute, Martina didn't think she would respond, but then she said, "For the record, I've been with Daniel for eight months. So get your facts straight!"

Carolyn hurried out of the room, but not before Martina saw her swipe angrily at her eyes. Normally a few words wouldn't affect her mother and Martina had to admit that she was a little surprised that they had this time. Had Caroline and Daniel really been dating eight months? Martina thought back, trying to recall the last time her mother was with someone else, but couldn't remember.

She turned to go back to the sink but stopped

when she looked up to find her grandmother's gaze on her.

"What?"

"I don't care what your mother does or how you disapprove of her lifestyle. You are *not* to disrespect her like that ever again. Do I make myself clear?" The no-nonsense tone and the fiery warning in her grandmother's eyes let Martina know she was serious, and the wrong answer might get her a smack across the mouth.

"Yes, ma'am."

Katherine Jenkins turned away and went back to spooning up the leftover collard greens, mumbling something Martina couldn't hear.

"So how does it taste?" Jada whispered close to Martina's ear but loud enough for everyone to probably hear.

"How's what taste?"

"That foot in your mouth."

Toni snickered, Christina's mouth twitched as if trying to hold in a laugh, but it was Peyton's disapproving frown that got Martina's attention.

Maybe she had gone too far this time.

"I need you girls to finish cleaning up in here before you leave," their grandmother finally spoke again. "And Martina I want you upstairs. Now," she added when Martina stood rooted in place staring at her.

"Gram, you do realize I don't live here anymore, right?" When Martina was young, being sent to her room was a norm. "You turned my room into a sewing room."

"You know what, Martina? I have had just about enough of your smart mouth today. Get upstairs, now!"

A short while later, Martina paced the length of her grandparent's den, that was connected to their bedroom. She stopped in front of the wall that housed photos of the family and zoomed in on one. The picture with her mother and her grandfather held her attention. At the time the photo was taken, Carolyn had been Martina's age, and the resemblance between mother and daughter was startling.

It's okay to look like her. I just don't want to be like her.

Martina glanced at the small clock on the table next to the loveseat, realizing she'd been waiting ten minutes. Hopefully, one of the guest would detain her grandmother, sparing Martina a tongue lashing.

Martina dropped into the chair closest to the window and stared out. Maybe she had been too hard on her mother over the last few years. But knowing she had been conceived because of an affair her mother had with a married man, disgusted Martina. The woman's so-called relationships since then hadn't been much better. As far as Martina knew, her mother hadn't hooked up with any more married men, but most of the men she dated were still losers. Except for maybe this latest boyfriend.

Martina glanced up when her grandmother strolled in, closing the door behind her. She tried not to groan at that stoic expression her grandmother rarely wore, but it was hard.

Might as well get this over with.

"I'm sorry, Gram, but you know how it is between her and me. She drives me nuts with her nonchalant, lackadaisical attitude. And if that's not bad enough, she's been married twice, each time ending up with a broken heart. Who wants to be a witness to that crap all the time?"

"Watch your mouth! I don't care how much you dislike your mother's choices. You still have to show her respect. For years, I have heard you go on and on about not wanting to be like her, but I don't think you realize just how much like Carolyn you are."

Martina shot out of her seat. "I am nothing like her! I'm not the one who keeps moving in with and falling in love with every man I meet. I'm not the one who keeps starting things and never finishing anything. And most importantly, I'm not the one who goes around sleeping with married men and having a child out of wedlock!"

"Sit down," her grandmother said softly after a frustrated sigh. When Martina didn't move, Katherine glanced up, her eyebrow lifted as if saying *did you hear me*.

Martina reclaimed her seat but diverted her gaze. Carolyn should have been the one getting a speech. As a matter of fact, she should have been given a good talking to years ago maybe after her second marriage.

"Your mother didn't know your father was married."

Martina jerked her head. "Excuse me?"

"She didn't know until you were conceived."

Martina's heart rate kicked up. Shock volleyed inside of her.

"How…how is that possible? Didn't she ever ask? What happened when she went over to his house? What did he do, hide all the family photos and lock his wife in the cellar? Was my mother that clueless?"

"When they were dating, he never told Carolyn he was married. From what I understand, they either met in her dorm room or his apartment. He didn't give her any reason to think that he wasn't single. When he found out she was pregnant, he insisted you weren't his and accused her of sleeping around."

"Had she been?"

Katherine shook her head. "She denied his accusations, and I believe her. That man deceived your mother. She was young and impressionable. He was much older. For over six months he wined and dined Carolyn, making her think he was in love with intentions of marriage. Then she got pregnant. Your father offered to pay for an abortion and when Carolyn didn't accept the money he disappeared."

Martina sat stunned. "Why didn't she tell me this? Why are you bringing it up now?"

"She's ashamed, MJ. Despite what you might think of your mother, she was a good girl. I never told you because I had hoped that one day you two could find some common ground and talk instead of arguing for a change. Now it seems your relationship with her is getting worse. I can't stand watching the way you two hurt each other. She's your mother. You're her daughter. There is no closer relationship."

A stab of guilt cut through Martina like lightening hitting metal, scorching every nerve within her. She couldn't believe her mother had gone through this and never told her.

"How did she find out this guy was married?"

"Your grandfather had planned to hunt him down and put a bullet in his head."

Martina gasped.

"Don't act so surprised. You know as well as I do that man would do anything for his family."

"So that's how my father died? Grampa killed

him?" Martina's hand rested over her heart, disbelief clouding her mind. She couldn't believe her grandfather had killed her father or anyone for that matter. Her mother had told her that her father died in a car accident.

"No, Steven didn't kill him. He hired a private investigator who found your father. Once your grandfather had the man's information, he went to see him. Put the fear of God in the guy." She shook her head and smiled as if mentally going back to that day. "Steven told him that if he ever approached Carolyn again, the authorities would find him at the bottom of the Ohio River. That's also when your grandfather found out he was married. Rodrick begged him not to tell his wife and your grandfather agreed but told him she would probably find out when he started paying child support."

Martina's head felt as if a storm was brewing inside her skull as she tried processing everything.

"My father's name was Rodrick?"

"His name *is* Rodrick Lachey. He lives in Dayton, Ohio."

"He's alive?"

Katherine nodded. "As far as we know. The only time you asked about your father was when you were four. I wanted to tell you everything, but your mother wanted him to remain dead to you."

"Why are you telling me this now?"

"Because it's way past time you knew and I want you to make things right with your mother. Life is short, sweetheart. You might not agree with the way she lives her life, but Carolyn loves you. She always has. She just doesn't know how to deal with you."

Martina knew she hadn't made it easy on her

mother. Guilt lodged in her gut. She had been a rambunctious child determined to drive Carolyn crazy.

Martina groaned and held the sides of her head, recalling some of the nasty things she had said over the years.

She should hate me.

"When Carolyn dropped out of college, she was working two jobs trying to take care of you. The child support helped, but it wasn't enough."

"So we moved in here," Martina finished. She sat back in the chair still trying to process everything she had learned.

"I said earlier that you and your mother are a lot alike. You're both kind-hearted, hard-working, loyal and … very stubborn. Must've taken that stubbornness after your grandfather." She spoke the last words without a smile, but Martina heard the humor in her voice. "Tomorrow is not guaranteed to any of us. Holding on to anger is never a good idea. As for that Ms. Independent attitude that you wear like a badge of honor, you're going to be a very lonely woman if you keep pushing people away. You've done it with your mother, and you're doing it with Paul. You and that mouth of yours just keeps getting in the way."

Paul.

Martina's heart throbbed thinking about how she'd been treating him. It wasn't just her mouth that was the problem, but also her attitude and fear of not being in control of her feelings when it came to him. She didn't know how to fix the problem. She didn't know how to fix herself.

"I think your mother falls in and out of

relationships because she longs for what she once shared with your father. Or what she thought she had."

"But does she have to marry them? I get sick of watching this ridiculous cycle with her, especially since she's always the one who gets hurt."

"Yes, but at least she has been brave enough to try out a relationship. And when they're over, she's strong enough to pull herself up, dust herself off and try again. Besides, the third time might be a charm." Her grandmother shrugged.

Yeah right.

"Martina, let me explain something else about your mother. Carolyn latches on to men who show an interest, hoping that he'll be the one to fill that void in her heart. Unlike you who has chosen the opposite route, not letting *any* man get too close."

Martina didn't bother asking how or what her grandmother knew about her relationships. Katherine Jenkins seemed to know everything about everyone in the family.

"I saw the way you and the Senator looked at each other a couple of weeks ago."

"What do you mean?"

"He's in love with you. And if I'm not mistaken, you're very much in love with him too."

Martina shook her head and stood. No way could her grandmother see that.

"Let me finish. Sweetheart, if you keep pushing him away or keep trying to keep him at arm's length, you might miss out on the best thing that has ever happened to you. Don't be afraid of love. I want all of my children and grandchildren to have what I have with your grandfather."

"There's not a man alive like Grampa."

Katherine laughed. "I agree. No one is like your Grampa, but I have a feeling that Senator of yours comes pretty close."

"Yeah, he does," Martina admitted remembering how she had been avoiding him and his phone calls.

What am I going to do about Paul?

CHAPTER THIRTEEN

"I'm done," Paul grumbled after leaving yet another message for Martina. In the last two weeks, she had avoided the majority of his calls.

He needed to have his head checked. Every night he went to sleep thinking about her. She dominated his dreams. And if that weren't enough, he woke to thoughts of her. Then the cycle started all over again.

Clearly he was suffering from some brain condition. That was the only reason he could come up with to explain why he hadn't moved on. He never had a problem attracting members of the opposite sex. Yet, there was only one woman who sparked something within him that he couldn't seem to walk away from.

"Yep. I need my head examined."

Paul strolled down the stairs and headed to the kitchen. After putting in some long days, it felt good to sit back on a Sunday evening and watch football. Knowing he didn't have to travel for the next four days made relaxing that much sweeter.

He pulled a beer from the refrigerator and a bag of chips from the pantry. When he decided to finally renovate the house, he hadn't thought about how long it would take to adjust to a larger place. Paul loved the house, but he wanted a home and a family.

The thought brought with it the last conversation between him and Martina about where she saw herself in five years. Paul wasn't ready to give up on her ... on them, but at some point, he would have to make some tough decisions if he planned to have a family. He wasn't getting any younger. If he were blessed with children, he wanted to still be able to chase after them.

Paul took the steps two at a time, returning to the den to watch the second half of the Cincinnati and Pittsburgh game. The moment he sat down and propped his feet on the ottoman, the doorbell rang.

He hurried back down the stairs, assuming it was Davion, but instead recognized Martina's figure through the textured glass door.

"Hey, wha…" His voice trailed off when she turned to him. The first thing he noticed were her red eyes and then the way she shivered, holding her jacket closed. "What happened? Are you okay?"

He reached for her hand and pulled her inside. Before he could say anything else, she dropped her bag and lunged into his arms. Her body trembled against him, and his protective instincts kicked in.

"Baby, you gotta tell me what happened. Are you hurt?" His heart pounding viciously, he tried loosening her grip from around his waist in order to see her face, but she held on tighter. "Martina, I need you to say something. Talk to me."

When she still didn't speak, he thought he heard

her sniffle. That couldn't be because he had never seen her cry. As a matter of fact, he was pretty sure there wasn't a vulnerable bone in her body.

"Martina."

"I just need you to hold me," she mumbled, her voice filled with emotion.

Okay, we're making progress.

He lifted her effortlessly in his arms, and she buried her face against his neck. Instead of returning to the den, he sat on the chaise lounge in the great room and held her against his body, brushing a kiss on her forehead.

He waited impatiently for her to say something. That smart mouth she used as a weapon, he could handle. Witnessing this side of her, he felt out of his element.

"I'm sorry," she finally said and tried to pull away, but he didn't release her. Finding her at his door looking despondent, scared the hell out of him. He held onto her more for himself than for her, wondering why she was apologizing. Maybe whatever was going on had to do with why she'd been avoiding him.

"Tell me what happened."

"It's been a tough afternoon." She wiped her face with the back of her hands. "And then my darn truck broke down and this stupid hill you live on almost killed me."

"Baby, why didn't you call me? I would have come and got you." It didn't matter that she hadn't returned the majority of his calls over the past couple of weeks. He would have gone to her.

"I needed the fresh air to help clear my mind. But I underestimated how steep and long that hill is. And

I didn't expect the temperature to drop to thirty-five degrees."

"That explains why you're shivering." He pulled her back against him and rubbed her arms, hoping to generate some heat. "Talk to me. What happened this afternoon?"

After a long hesitation, Martina related her encounter with her mother and the lecture she received from her grandmother. Once she finished telling him everything, they sat in silence except for the upstairs television, which he could barely hear.

"Despite my grandparents encouraging my mother to stay in school and them offering to help with me, she didn't go back. When I was about two, we moved in with them, and I saw less and less of my mother. She was always gone or working, or falling in and out of love. By the time I was in high school, I didn't want to have anything to do with her. Our relationship has continued to decline since."

She sat up but didn't move from Paul's lap. He ran his fingers through her soft hair the way he used to do, loving how silky it felt. He also loved that she had come to him. Her stubborn, independent attitude kept her from asking anything of him. So he knew showing up on his doorstep hadn't been easy for her.

"What happened between you and your mother during your high school years to make you distance yourself?"

"By the time I was a freshman, she was on her second husband. The same as her first marriage, when I was in middle school, she gave me a choice to move in with them or stay with my grandparents."

"You chose your grandparents," he said more as a statement than a question. He wished he would have had a choice like that. He would have chosen to live with his grandparents too.

"Actually, my grandparents chose me, feeling they could keep a better eye on me. My mother didn't argue, and I would have chosen them anyway. They had more love for me in their little finger than my mother could ever muster."

"Do you really believe that?"

She sighed and laid back against him. "Yes. No. I don't know what to believe anymore. My mother is flaky. Never finishes anything she starts. Not parenthood, college or anything else from what I can see. I vowed a long time ago that I would be nothing like her. She falls in love at a drop of a hat and then gets dumped. A couple of months later, the cycle starts all over again."

Now Paul had a better understanding, regarding her resistance to love and commitment. He just wasn't sure what to do with this new knowledge. There had to be a way to show her she should take a chance on him. On them.

"So why were you crying when you arrived?"

"I wasn't crying," she lied. "Some crap flew in my eyes while I was walking here."

"Uh huh," was all he could say without laughing at her tough-guy attitude.

"My grandmother's speech hit its target. Sometimes it's not easy to hear unfavorable things about yourself."

"Were they true?"

"Yeah, unfortunately. You probably don't know this, but I'm good at pushing people away. I also shy away from long-term relationships."

"Nooo, I would have never guessed."

They both laughed, but she quickly sobered.

"Gramma told me that if I didn't straighten, I was going to be a very lonely woman in my old age. No one wants a relationship with someone who is mean and judgmental." She sat quietly before adding, "She didn't say that last part, but she might as well had because it's true."

Paul held her tighter, glad that she felt comfortable enough to share what was on her mind.

"That scared me." She pulled away and stood, pacing away from him. "Peyton, Toni and the rest of them are my everything. I survived life because of them. Now that most of them are married or in relationships, we don't spend as much time together."

Paul remained quiet, wondering where this conversation was going, but feeling a twinge of hope. Maybe she was finally ready to acknowledge that there was something real between them.

"How do you feel about that?"

She looked up at him, tears lacing her eyelashes. "I'm scared. I don't want to be alone, but I don't want to be like my mother who changes relationships as often as some women change nail polish."

She dropped her head into her hands, and he thought he heard her sob. This was a different, softer side of Martina.

Paul stood and approached her knowing he was going to have to be careful in how he moved forward in their relationship. He wanted her, all of her, but he didn't want her to be with him only because she was concerned about growing old alone.

He lifted her chin with the pad of his finger, forcing those beautiful brown eyes to look at him.

"What can I do? What do you need from me?"

She swiped at her tears with the back of her hand, but they came just as fast.

She shook her head, her arms were wrapped around herself as if she were still cold. "I don't know. I don't know what I need right now."

"Okay." He pulled her into his arms and kissed the top of her head. "Come on. Let's go upstairs. You can take a hot shower and warm up while I find you something to eat."

*

Martina watched Paul's every move as he pulled items out of the refrigerator. She liked seeing him when he dressed down. Cincinnati Football was stamped on the front of the t-shirt that stretched across his wide chest. The perfectly worn jeans that hung low on his hips made him look ruggedly handsome.

Hot and sexy were the best words to describe him. At forty, he still had a body that could rival a man in his twenties.

Paul turned to catch her staring at him, but instead of speaking, he winked, sending heat spreading through her body. She didn't stand a chance at fighting the never ending attraction they shared if a wink could get her all hot and bothered.

Why had she showed up on his doorstep? The plan was to go home, curl up with a bag of potato chips and watch football for the rest of the night. But her truck had a mind of its own and steered itself to Mt. Adams.

She folded her arms on the counter top and lowered her head. Pathetic. That's what she was. This remarkable, patient man doted on her despite her stupidity and inability to commit. Why couldn't she just tell him how she felt? That she loved him.

He deserved so much more.

Her grandmother's words rattled around in her head. Everything she'd said to Martina had been on point, but Martina hadn't been prepared to hear the truth.

She also hadn't missed the disappointment radiating in her grandmother's eyes first in the kitchen and then again upstairs in the bedroom. All Martina wanted was for her mother to step up and stop allowing men to use her. She wanted a mother she could be proud of. She wanted a mother she *should* be proud of.

Martina startled when a hand landed on her shoulder.

"Eat before your food gets cold," Paul said nodding toward the plate that he had set down in front of her.

The smell of oregano, basil, and tomato sauce tickled her nose and her mouth watered at the sight of the plate of lasagna. She hadn't eaten much at the brunch. Her stomach had been in knots about what to do about Paul.

Now thoughts of her mother wreaked havoc in her mind. Martina owed her a huge apology for her behavior over the years. Unfortunately, saying *I'm sorry* didn't come easy.

Paul pushed the plate closer to Martina.

"Eat."

Her gaze took in the cheesy lasagna and her stomach growled in anticipation.

"My favorite," she mumbled and accepted the fork from Paul. She took a bite, closed her eyes and groaned. The man could cook for her any day.

"You know you say that about everything I cook. How am I going to know which meal is your real favorite?" He sat next to her and opened two beers, placing one near her plate.

"Everything you cook is my favorite," she responded honestly over a mouthful of food. She knew some men who cooked well, but none like Paul. He'd often talked about going to culinary school and then opening a restaurant. But as far as she was concerned, he didn't need schooling. The man was a natural born chef.

Martina ate while he nursed his beer. No doubt he was waiting for her to talk more about the tears that caught even her off guard. He probably also wanted a better explanation of why she was there, especially after she'd been avoiding him.

Martina wasn't sure what to say. She wasn't one of those crying women, but leaving her grandparent's home, she hadn't realized just how heavy her heart had been until she pulled out of the driveway. Before she knew it, she was on her way to Paul.

She continued eating in silence. Paul's patience with her should qualify him for sainthood, making her love him that much more.

When Martina finished eating, she and Paul snuggled together on the over-sized sofa in his den. She shivered beneath the blanket he'd given her the moment they sat down.

"Why do you have it so cold in this room?"

Paul's lips quirked. "So that whenever you're here, you'll be forced to sit close to me."

She stared at him and burst out laughing. "Is that the best you can do? Surely that line doesn't work on other women."

"If you haven't figured it out by now, there is no other woman for me."

Gazing into his eyes, her heart split open with what she felt for him. She cupped his cheek, the pad of her thumb caressing the short stubble.

"I love you, Paul."

She was so glad he didn't say anything. His head lowered, and her toes curled at the slow, passionate kiss that had her whimpering for more.

God, she loved this man.

Happiness filled her, and no other words were needed. Since coming back into her life, he had shared his feelings for her and had shown her too.

Martina needed to decide how much of herself she was ready to give to him. But right now, she didn't want to talk or think. All she wanted to do was get lost in the love that she felt just being in his arms.

*

Paul held Martina in the crook of his arm as they lay snuggled on his sofa. He was glad she had come to him. They still hadn't talked about where to go from there, but he'd been patient this long, there was no harm in waiting a little longer.

"What are you thinking about?" he asked, running his hand up and down her arm. Her skin so soft, he couldn't stop touching her.

"I think I want us to be more than friends with benefits."

Paul's breath stalled in his chest and seconds ticked by before he was able to exhale. Had he not been lying down, her words would have knocked him on his butt.

All this time, he had craved her like an addict craved his next fix, and she was finally his. Although there was something still a little unsettling about her tone. Still some insecurity. He had a feeling there was going to be more to her statement. He'd known her long enough to know that nothing came easily with her.

She didn't expound, and he remained quiet. Snuggled close to his side, Martina made small circles on his chest with the tip of her finger.

She glanced up at him. "I do have a few conditions."

And there it was.

Paul brought her small hand to his mouth and kissed the back of each finger before speaking.

"Martina, I'm not negotiating for love. You know how I feel about you, and I finally know how you feel about me. You're either in this with me or not. There won't be any of this one foot in and one foot out in this relationship. So what's it going to be? You in … or are you out?"

He rested her hand on his chest, covering it with his.

Their gazes met and held.

Come on baby. Give me a chance. Give us a chance.

"I'm in."

CHAPTER FOURTEEN

Paul entered the gate code at the entry of his parent's estate in Indian Hill. He had flown into Cincinnati an hour ago and figured he would head straight to their home since his mother insisted on seeing him. Paul had called her a couple of times before leaving the airport, hoping that whatever she wanted to see him about could be covered in a telephone conversation. He should have known she would ignore his calls. When Angelica Kendricks summoned you, you went.

Paul drove around the semi-circular drive and stopped in front of the brick, seven bedroom, ten bathroom home where he and his two sisters had grown up. He shut off the engine and took in the two-story, castle-like home that sat on five plus acres. The elegant, European manor-style building was his mother's pride and joy, fitting the bigger than life image she insisted on flaunting.

Workers were out front hanging Christmas lights. It was early November, but his mother always wanted the home decorated before the holiday season. Soon she would be full steam ahead in the numerous parties she hosted between then and the New Year.

Paul sighed.

"Might as well get this over with." The moment he stepped out of his vehicle, the front double doors opened.

A smile lifted the corners of his lips. "Hey Janice. You sure are a sight for sore eyes." He hugged the woman who had been more like a mother than a housekeeper to him since he was eight years old.

"Oh stop, you sweet talker." She greeted him with a kiss on the cheek like always. "Come on in. Your mother stepped out for a minute, but she says she'll be back shortly."

Paul closed the doors. He walked past the semi-spiral staircase and crossed the large, marble foyer, following Janice into the kitchen.

"It smells like you've been baking." Paul sat at the breakfast bar that overlooked the state of the art kitchen. Many days he had sat in the same spot while Janice roamed around the kitchen preparing one of her masterpiece meals. She had been the one to spark his interest in cooking. Once his grandfather noticed his interest, he encouraged Paul by teaching him to cook.

"You look tired," Janice said instead of responding to his comment about baking. "Have you been sleeping?" She stood before him, hands resting on her plump hips.

Paul didn't bother lying. He always thought Janice could read his mind.

"Not much. I've been pretty busy these last few weeks." He didn't tell her he hadn't been able to sleep because a certain, cutie-pie carpenter had been occupying his mind and his bed whenever he was in town.

"So who is she?"

Paul's eyebrows shot up. "Huh?"

"You heard me." She strolled away and brought over a familiar container and sat it in front of him. "I recognize the look."

Paul chuckled, his gaze on the covered dish knowing what was under the lid.

"I swear I think you're a mind reader."

She lifted the lid and set it aside. His mouth watered at the site of his favorite cookies, Pecan Sandies.

Biting into one, he shook his head and chuckled again. This was how she always got him to talk about his problems when he was a kid, like when he'd been bullied in grade school. Or the time in high school when Cheris Jones dumped him during sophomore year, the day before homecoming. Janice's listening ear and her Pecan Sandies got him through those rocky times.

"So how do you do it?" Paul asked as she pulled a roasting pan out of the oven.

"When it's a girl that's on your mind, or should I say a woman in this case, you have a little twinkle in your eye. Even exhaustion can't hide it." She dropped her oven mitts on the counter near the stove and sat next to him. "So who is she?"

Paul bit into his second cookie debating on how much to tell the family's housekeeper who was his childhood confidant. What could he tell her? That he was deeply in love with a woman he thought he had gotten over a year ago? A woman who had finally agreed to a serious relationship, but still seemed to be holding back.

"Is this the same woman who broke your heart about a year ago?"

Paul's eyebrows dipped as he turned to Janice. "What? How? I haven't mentioned one woman to you since before high school graduation. What makes you think someone dumped me?"

"I didn't say she dumped you. I said she broke your heart. So is this the same woman?"

"Yes." He turned back to the cookie container. The last thing he wanted to do was get full on cookies, especially since he and Martina had plans for dinner later, but the Pecan Sandies were a welcome treat. "She's the woman for me, but I'm not sure she's ready for the life I want with her, though she claims she is."

He shared how he and Martina ran into each other two months earlier, as well as how he hired Jenkins & Sons Construction to do the renovations on his home.

Once he was done telling his story, they sat in silence.

"If she's the woman you can see growing old with, don't give up on her. She must be very special for you to go through so much to get her attention.

Paul chuckled. She was special all right.

Just then, his mother breezed into the room like a category seven hurricane. She looked as if she'd just stepped out of one of the stores on Fifth Avenue in New York City, her home away from home. By the chic black and gray dress she had on, and her hair falling in curls around her shoulders, it was safe to say she had just returned from an outing with some of her girlfriends. He could usually tell where she'd been based on her outfit, hair and which diamonds she pulled out of her jewelry box.

"Oh good. I'm glad you're here," she said by way of greeting. She went straight to the refrigerator and pulled out a bottle of water. "Oh and Janice, we won't be home for dinner tonight."

Janice acknowledged the comment with a bow of her head and went back to work in the kitchen.

Paul hated when his parents did this. No regard for the fact that Janice always prepared elaborate meals which often took more than a few hours of work. Instead of informing her days in advance or even that morning that they had plans for dinner, they would tell her an hour before dinner was to be served.

"Hello, mother."

"Oh hi dear." She gave a slight wave as if saying hello had been an afterthought. "We're having an all-black cocktail party here, two weeks from Friday, and I need you to be here."

"Why?" He grabbed yet another cookie hoping its sweetness could dull the sudden bitterness in his mouth. His mother was notorious for theme parties or parties period. And he didn't know why he bothered sitting there waiting for her to ask something of him that Paul was sure he wouldn't want to do.

"We're having a few people over, and many of them are your constituents. It's time we start thinking seriously about the presidency and—"

"Stop." Paul wiped his mouth and stood. "I'm not doing this tonight. I don't know how many times I have to tell you and dad that I'm not interested in running for president."

"Oh Paul, quit being so dramatic. I'm not saying you have to run in the next election, but thinking about the presidency is the next step for you, dear."

Paul walked over to Janice and kissed her on the cheek. "Thanks for the cookies and for listening," he whispered close to her ear.

Good luck she mouthed before he pulled away.

Of course, his mother was oblivious to the whole exchange as she stared down at her cell phone.

"Bye mother." He moved past her and headed for the entrance of the kitchen.

"Paul."

Before she could say more, the doorbell rang.

Janice excused herself to get the door, and a weird feeling swirled around Paul. He glanced at his mother who positioned herself in a kitchen chair. She crossed her leg, her modest heeled shoe dangling from her foot as if she didn't have a care in the world.

People rarely stopped by without his mother's knowledge. Not only that, normally she would be fixing her hair or adjusting her clothes, making sure she looked perfect.

"What are you up to, Mother?"

"I don't know what—"

"Mrs. Kendricks, Mrs. Chambers, and her daughter are here to see you," Janice said when she reentered the kitchen. "I put them in the study, but would you prefer I show them to the kitchen?"

"The study is fine, Janice."

Paul shook his head. "You are a real piece of work. Trying to ambush me. I'm not sticking around for this. I'm outta here."

"Paul please." His mother touched his arm. "Don't leave like this. I just want you to meet Antoinette.

She's a lovely woman, who I think you'll like."

"Mother, how many times do I have to tell you that I don't need, nor do I want you fixing me up with any of your friends' daughters?"

"I don't always set you up, but that's beside the point. You can't keep attending these events solo, and when you do, at least, talk to some of the women. Soon people will think that yo—"

"I don't care what people think. I'm not interested in any of the women you think are right for me."

"Dear, you are continuing the family's political dynasty and will need a good, well-bred woman by your side. At least, meet her. Besides, it wouldn't be nice for you to walk out without at least saying hello."

Mention of the family political dynasty made him want to walk out the door and not look back.

"I'm sorry, Mother. I have plans for this evening and need to run a few errands before then."

She followed behind him as he headed to the front door, but before he could leave, two women stepped into the doorway of the study. One he recognized as his mother's friend. The other he assumed was her daughter.

"Paul, you remember, Gladis Chambers, don't you?"

"Hello, Mrs. Chambers. Nice to see you again."

"You too, Paul. I'd like for you to meet my daughter, Antoinette. She's in town for a few weeks before returning to Maryland."

"Nice to meet you," Paul said shaking Antoinette's hand.

"You too, Senator. I've heard a lot about you."

"Please call me Paul."

"Paul it is."

Her seductive tone and the way her hungry gaze raked down the length of him was an immediate turnoff. Not that he would have been interested anyway. She was tall for a woman with a pretty face and a fit body, but she wasn't what he wanted in his life. She wasn't Martina.

"Well, it's been nice seeing you both, but I have to get going."

"Oh, I was hoping we could get to know each other better. I'm very interested in your position on gun control as well as the bill you proposed regarding educational funding. I had hoped to hear more about your political stand on the subjects."

Paul almost laughed out loud. Maybe he should be interested in a person who supported his work. All he could think about was the feisty woman across town who thought his political spiel was hogwash.

"Sorry, I can't stay. My girlfriend is probably wondering what's taking me so long." He felt a little pleased with himself at his mother's gasp. "Maybe I'll see you here in a couple of weeks at the party. Until then, you ladies take care." He glanced over his shoulder. "Mother," he said and headed for the door, not stopping until she called out to him, his hand on the doorknob.

"Paul, wait." A smile flitted across his mother's lips. "Why didn't you tell me you were seeing someone? Who is she?" She snapped her finger, not giving him a chance to respond. Though he wasn't sure, he was ready to tell her about Martina. "I know. Its Elizabeth, Congressman Moody's daughter, isn't it? I noticed her interest in you this summer at her father's barbecue, but I'm surprised you're interested in her. She came across as a little pushy and insincere.

Who would want to be with someone like that?"

"Yeah, why would I—"

"Don't you have somewhere to be, Paul?" Janice chimed in. He hadn't seen her near the stairs.

Paul smiled when he met her gaze. She must have sensed that he was about to tell his mother that Elizabeth was too much like her for him to ever be interested. It probably was best to leave that conversation alone.

"You're right, Ms. Janice. I should be going. Goodbye, mother." He opened the door and stepped outside.

"Just make sure you're here for the party … with a date." His mother said to his back. "I mean it, Paul."

As far as Paul was concerned, he was only attending the party with one person. And he knew she'd rather drive a nail into her hand before she rubbed shoulders with the type of people who would be in attendance.

Paul smiled to himself as he drove away from the house. If he decided to ask Martina, and she said yes, he knew he'd have a good time. But would she say yes?

*

"Heck no, I don't want to attend some stuffy party at your parents' house. Are you crazy? Can you see me, at a party with your constituents?" Martina said and took their coats to the closet.

Martina shook her head as she hung their garments on hangers. She didn't know if she was ready to be on display? She was just getting used to them being an official couple and now this.

While they were at dinner, he seemed preoccupied. He might have been thinking about the party, but she suspected something else was bothering him.

When Paul didn't speak, she glanced over her shoulder to find him smiling

"What?" She walked across the room and plopped down on the sofa next to him, stretching her legs across his thighs. "What's with the smile?"

"I'm just imagining you at that party." He shook his head. "That probably wouldn't be a good idea."

"I'm surprised you mentioned it."

"I'm surprised too, especially since I know how you feel about those types of events. And before you start freaking out, I don't have any preconceived notions that you're going to be suddenly interested in integrating into that part of my world. A world that I'm not even sure, I want to remain in."

Martina shifted next to him, sliding her legs beneath her. "What does you not remaining in that world mean?"

"It means that I've had enough. I have allowed my parents to live vicariously through me. Our family has always been in politics, but I'm a third generation U.S. Senator and my parents assume that I plan to stay in politics until I retire, the way my grandfather had."

Martina placed her feet on the floor and moved closer, waiting for him to say more.

"Despite the way I make them sound like a nightmare, I do love them. It's just that the last few years they've become almost unbearable when it comes to *my* career, especially my mother. She has big dreams for me, but I'm tired. Tired of living my life for them and as long as I stay in politics, that's exactly, what I'm doing."

"Have you told them how you feel?"

He chuckled bitterly. "You have to know my

mother to understand how funny that question is. She hears what she wants to hear and me not making a run for the White House is not something she wants to hear. It probably doesn't help that I showed an interest in politics when I was a kid."

"How old were you?"

"Six." Paul wrapped his arm around her shoulder and pulled her closer to his side. "I wanted to be like my grandfather and my father. They made the political scene seem exciting. I liked that they wanted to be a part of history and make a positive difference in people's lives. But politics is so much bigger. The constant battles within and between political parties, the number of events and all of the traveling has gotten old. My heart isn't in it anymore. I've been thinking more and more about opening a restaurant."

Martina interlocked her hand with his, debating about what to say. He was an outstanding cook and crazy smart so she could easily see him starting a restaurant. And though she always gave him a hard time about his political position, she knew he had a good heart.

"Are you sure that's what you want to do?" she finally asked. "You've made a difference in the Senate. Maybe you shouldn't be too hasty in leaving."

With a raised eyebrow, he turned to her. "I would think you of all people would be happy that S*atan's spawn* is thinking about hanging up his political hat. Isn't that what you want?"

She regretted she had ever called him that.

"Baby, it doesn't matter what I want. Question is, is this what you want? I'll admit that you're good at what you do." When his eyebrows went higher, she continued. "Don't go getting a big head, I still don't like all the crap you spew, but you mean a lot to me. As quiet as it's kept, I want you to be happy."

The left side of his beautiful mouth quirked and a full 100-watt smile spread across his kissable lips.

"So I mean a lot to you, huh." He ran the back of his fingers slowly down her cheeks, and she leaned into his touch. "I want us both to be happy." His voice went deeper. The emotion in his tone and the way his large hand slid down the side of her body, sending sweet tingles to every nerve ending, said way more than his words. "And since I know something that would make both of us happy, why don't—"

"Hold up." She squirmed beneath him, feeling his erection press against her hip. "Before you start getting all touchy-feely, let's get back to this party. For you to have brought it up, knowing how I feel about these types of events must mean it's important to you."

After a long hesitation he said, "I need you to go as my date. It's a matter of life or death."

She squinted at him trying to figure out if he were serious, but then she noticed the twinkle in his eyes. "Whose life...or death?"

"Mine...or my mother's," he said with a straight face. Martina grinned at how cute he looked while trying to pretend seriousness. "If you don't go with me, she's going to fix me up with her friend's daughter."

The smile slipped from Martina's face. "So rich people really do that kind of stuff? I thought that was just in the movies or in those mushy romance novels."

Paul chuckled, playing with her hair. Martina was enjoying their times together, especially moments like this. She never thought she would get into lounging around the house, talking like a couple planning to attend their next event or outing.

"I can't speak for other wealthy families," Paul interrupted her thoughts, "but my mother feels it's her duty to find me a women who she thinks will make a good first lady. She's determined to get into the White House. And since my father didn't make it, I'm her only chance."

Martina thought she had problems with her mother. Their differences were nothing compared to what it sounded like Paul had to deal with when it came to his mother.

"I'm sure this party is my mother's way of pushing her agenda. She has their friends and my constituents thinking like her. But I plan to make it loud and clear at the party that I won't be running for another term in the Senate or anything else for that matter."

"Apparently, I'm going to have to teach you how to deal with difficult parents. By the time I'm done with you, you'll be able to say something to them one time, and they'll know you mean business."

Paul laughed and pulled Martina close and placed a kiss against the side of her forehead. "That's why I need you in my life."

He turned her in his arms until their lips touch. He nipped at her top lip, then her bottom. Martina's pulse thumped wildly, and her senses exploded when he took full control of her mouth.

A guttural moan slipped from her throat and her slender arms coiled easily around his neck. Yeah, she needed him in her life too, especially when his skilled mouth pressed against her lips and did wicked things to her whole body.

"I'll go to the party with you," she said panting. She unbuttoned her blouse, letting it slide down her arms and onto the floor.

Paul's arms snaked behind her, quickly undoing her bra. "Did I hear you correctly?" He nuzzled her neck and worked his way down nipping at her skin. "You'll go to my parents' house with me?" he mumbled against the top of her breasts as he palmed them between his hands.

"You heard right," she said, barely able to think with him teasing her nipples with the pads of his thumb.

He lifted his head, and their eyes met. "Why the change of heart?"

"Because I'll be damn if I'm going to let your mother try and hook you up with some prissy little debutante. You're mine." She cupped his smiling face between her hands. "Besides, it's about time she and I met."

"I couldn't agree more." He kissed her softly before standing, pulling her up with him. "God, I love you." He palmed her butt and lifted her into his arms. Her legs wound around his waist and he headed toward the bedroom.

"And I love you."

A month ago, she couldn't say those words out loud. Now they flowed like water and she meant them. Sometimes the fear of rejection and fear of ending up like her mother reared its wicked head, but no way was she letting fear win out any longer. She and Paul belonged together, and Martina had every intention of keeping it that way.

CHAPTER FIFTEEN

The day before the Kendricks' party, Martina and Peyton showed up at Jada's house, the go-to person when it came to fashion.

"All I want to know is, can I attend this party with you?" Jada asked as she led them into her closet, which was a spare bedroom.

Martina had no idea why one person needed this many clothes, shoes and everything else that could be found in the women's section at Bloomingdales. Heck, the space looked like a department store. Long racks of clothes lined the perimeter of the large space while accessories were displayed on tall tables in the center of the room.

Martina strolled across the room to the boots section. She picked up a pair of purple suede, thigh-high boots.

"Really, Jada? Where do you even wear something like this?"

"MJ, don't start."

Martina put the boots back. "Oh and as far as the

Kendricks' party, I'm sure they won't have a problem with you attending. Though you'll probably have a better chance of getting in if Zack is with you."

Zack was the city's golden boy. Everyone loved him. Not only had he been one of the greatest running backs of his time, he also supported numerous nonprofit organizations.

"I'll keep that in mind. I only want to go because I want to watch you do something outlandish that will probably land you on the cover of the society page."

"I plan to be on my best behavior. Just show me the dresses." This was one of those days when she was glad they wore the same size. Since being married, Jada, thanks to Zack, had put a little meat on her bones. No longer able to wear a size two or four or whatever she used to wear. She now owned sizes six and eight. Perfect for Martina.

"Before you say anything, I'm not giving you a black outfit," Jada pulled three dresses from one of the built in cabinets.

"I'm only wearing black because I only have black pumps. And there is no way in hell I'm wearing a pair of your break-your-damn-neck heels."

"Do you know how much I spend on shoes?"

"Yes, I do. Before Zack came along, we were the ones who had to suffer through your shopping sprees."

"Well, then you should know me well enough to know that I'm not letting anyone wear my shoes, especially you." She moved to another cabinet and pulled out several boxes of shoes. "That's why I bought you your own to go with the dresses. Ones that will hold up if you decided to take one off your foot and hit someone with it. Or if you decided to kick them off and *leave them* at the party."

"That happened one time, Jada. Almost ten years ago! Why are you even bringing that up?" Back when Martina and Peyton were in their early twenties, they had attended a party, and Martina had let Peyton talk her into wearing heels. They had danced all night until Martina eventually kicked off the shoes. When the party was raided by the cops, she ran out of the house, leaving the shoes behind.

Martina turned to Peyton and glared. "As a matter of fact, *Jada*, how did you know about that since you were too young to hang out with us back then?"

Peyton lifted her hands. "Don't look at me. I didn't tell her."

"It doesn't matter. Let's get this party started. Take a look at the dresses and tell me what you think." Jada laid the outfits on a dressing table.

Martina folded her arms. "I don't like 'em. They're not black."

"Everyone is going to be wearing black to this event *except* Paul's mother. Based on what you've told us about her, she'll probably wear red."

Martina and Peyton stared at Jada until Peyton spoke.

"What makes you think she won't wear black?"

"Because I wouldn't. I would wear red, especially if I told everyone else it was an all-black affair."

She said it as if her words made perfect sense.

Martina shook her head. "I don't care about all of that. Just find me a cute, simple, black dress."

"No. These are your choices. MJ you always march to your own beat, doing your own thing. This is a perfect opportunity to show this group who you are and how you operate. Besides, you and Paul are going pretty hot and heavy these days. Mommy Dearest needs to get used to seeing you and know that she has no power over you. So you might as well stand out when you make your entrance. I always do." Jada lifted an eyebrow, her hands on her narrow hips as if waiting for Martina, to deny anything she had said.

Martina folded her lower lip between her teeth and studied the dresses. Jada was right about one thing. She always marched to her own beat. She also wanted to make it clear to all the single hussies with plans to get their hooks into Paul that he wasn't available.

"Red, light gray, or baby blue, which is it going to be?" Jada asked after she held each one up for her review.

"Which would you recommend?" Martina asked.

"The red one … or the light blue. Red always stands out and catches attention. And since the dress is long with this serious split up the side, all heads will turn when you step into that house." She lifted the light blue one again. "Now this little number will show your no-fear attitude. It'll stop just above your knee and with the high collar, it'll make your boobs look twice their size. Oh and if that doesn't get attention, when you walk pass, all mouths will fall open when they see the back." She turned the outfit around, and Martina's mouth dropped open.

"Dang, Jada. These look more like your taste, not mine. Don't you have a cute little tuxedo for women somewhere in this department store?"

"I do, but you're not wearing it. These are your choices. So what's it going to be?"

Martina sighed dramatically and had thought about closing her eyes and just pointing at one. She needed the perfect dress.

"Here. Try this on." Jada shoved the red gown into Martina's hands.

Peyton, who hadn't said much up to this point, finally spoke.

"I can't believe I'm going to say this, but I agree with Jada. Well except the part about you not wearing black. If it's an all-black event, you wear black. *Wait.*" She held her hands out when both Jada and Martina started to speak, "There's something else you need to be mindful of."

"And what would that be?" Martina grabbed the red dress and shoes. She took the items behind the elaborate dressing screen that stood in a nearby corner.

"Paul is a U.S. Senator. You are not only there to stake your claim, but you're there to support him. You are a reflection of him and just as important, you know what Grampa always says. Wherever you go, whatever you do, you're representing the Jenkins family."

"So whatever you do, don't go in there acting a fool," Jada added.

"Like you did at the breakfast that day," Peyton said as if Martina needed a reminder of how she had run off at the mouth.

Martina shook out of her button down shirt as she thought about the speech her grandfather had given her after that incident.

She shivered at the memory of seeing Steven Jenkins that angry. He had told her if she ever showed her tail the way she had that day, disrespecting a Senator or anyone else, not only would she not ever attend an event representing the family business, but she would be looking for a new job.

She didn't know how he found out everything because she knew Peyton hadn't said a word. All she knew was that he had heard enough to almost quote every word she had spoken in that banquet room.

Martina wiggled into the dress as she remembered another time her grandfather had been that angry. It was that night when Toni was arrested at a drug house. The scene of her arrest had been blasted on every local television channel. And of course, the media had everything wrong. Had it not been for Craig, who was a police detective, there was no telling how long it would have taken to clear Toni's name.

"Any day now, MJ. What's taking you so long? Let's see the dress." The impatience in Jada's tone resonated loud and clear.

Martina turned to the full-length mirror and took in the sleeveless gown that wrapped around every curve making her appear more voluptuous than she thought possible. The sparkling beads on the shoulders and down the sides of the dress reminded her of diamonds, and all Martina could do was stand there and stare.

"Come on already, MJ! Don't make me come back there!"

Most of the Jenkins girls lacked patience and Jada was the worse.

Martina stepped from behind the screen feeling like Cinderella and smoothed her hands down the front of the soft, flowing material.

"So, what do you guys think?"

Jada squealed. "The red it is. You are going to blow Paul away!"

"Oh. My. God." Peyton gawked as if not recognizing her. "Though I think Jada gave you terrible advice about not wearing black, you look incredible in that dress.

Martina wanted to look good for Paul, but he was only part of her agenda. Since his mother was into matchmaking, Martina needed her and every woman in attendance to take notice. Paul was no longer on the market, and she planned to make it clear that they were together. She just hoped no one tried to challenge her. Otherwise, Paul might be sorry he asked her to be his date.

*

Paul adjusted his bow-tie as he strolled up the walkway that led to Martina's small bungalow. For the past couple of weeks, he waited for the call informing him she had changed her mind and couldn't attend. It never came.

Back together for a few months now, Paul was glad that she finally seemed comfortable with them being a couple.

He rang the doorbell, and shuffled side to side, rubbing his hands together. The November chill in full effect tonight went straight through his jacket. He turned to find the driver that he'd hired for the evening, still standing comfortably near the back door of the car as if it weren't ridiculously windy and twenty-eight degrees outside.

Paul reached to ring the doorbell again, but before he could, the door swung open. His words lodged in his throat. His pulse amped up as he took in the statuesque beauty standing before him, loving the transformation. With curls piled on top of her head and a few tendrils framing her perfectly made up face, Martina could have easily graced the cover of any fashion magazine. His gaze went lower, taking in the form fitted evening gown that wrapped around her curves like a second skin. Then he noticed the deep split up the side of the dress that not only revealed a shapely leg, but a firm thigh that...

"Are you just going to stand there? Or are you going to say something?" Martina grabbed his attention with her playful tone, a soft smile on her face and a mischievous glint in her eyes.

"I...I...*damn*, baby." He stepped forward but didn't walk into the house. He lifted her arm up, twirling her in a circle to get a good look at the entire gown. "You're absolutely breathtaking." He almost added that her firm, shapely ass had his mouth watering, but kept that thought to himself.

Never had he seen her look so feminine. She was sexy in anything she wore, but they were surely going to attend more black-tie affairs if it meant seeing her all dolled up in evening wear.

"Paul, it's cold out there, and you have the door open. Are you coming in or do you want to wait out there until I get my wrap?"

Blown away by her appearance, he hadn't realized he was still standing on the outside. The spark she lit inside of him was strong enough to start a forest fire, and he knew if he touched her again, they were going to be late.

He stepped across the threshold but stayed near the door while trying to get his body under control. Inhaling and exhaling slowly was doing very little to tamp down the desire roaring through his body. He felt like a horny teenager on prom night, anxious for the dance to be over so he could see what was beneath his date's dress.

"All right, I'm ready."

His gaze soaked her up as she glided toward him. He was the luckiest man alive to have this woman on his arm tonight, and she was going home with him.

"So is there anything I should know before we get there. Anything I should *not* say in front of the people you guys are expecting to be there? I've already been given speeches by Jada and Peyton to keep my mouth closed and look cute, but is there anything you want to add?"

"You look stunning." He pulled her against his body, her softness molding against him. "You are a phenomenal woman who I absolutely adore. I want you to just be yourself."

She cocked a perfectly arched brow. "You sure about that?"

"Positive. Let's go. We're going to have a great time."

CHAPTER SIXTEEN

Martina almost whistled when the driver pulled onto the Kendricks' estate. Though it was nighttime, the property was well lit, putting on full display the manicured grounds with full-grown trees and lush flowerbeds.

Her grandparents' estate was impressive, but this family's wealth showed without her even having to know their net worth or step foot into their home.

The sprawling mansion came into view, spotlights highlighting the magnificent structure as well as the fountain. This time she did whistle, not caring that it wasn't very ladylike. Jada had given her a crash course in etiquette and another speech about acting like a woman. Martina had to admit she appreciated her cousin's efforts and now wished she had paid better attention.

"So this is where you grew up, huh?"

"Yes, this is it." He squeezed her hand. "Maybe before we leave, I can give you a tour."

"Now that's an offer I wouldn't turn down."

As the Town Car jumped in line behind several other cars that were just arriving, Martina took it all in. French Normandy architectural design made the home look more like a palace. She had always been infatuated with homes and architecture and this one didn't disappoint.

Moments later, they stood in the huge marble foyer. There was so much to see, Martina couldn't decide where to train her eyes. The impressive semi-spiral staircase, the ornamental columns that gave the open space a regal appearance or on the floor to ceiling windows that were straight ahead and took up a wall that had to be a least twenty-feet long.

Make sure you don't act as if you're not used to anything. Jada's words came to mind when Martina realized her mouth was hanging open as she turned in a full circle taking in the foyers cathedral ceiling.

From the open foyer, Martina realized that she and Paul had captured the attention of many of the guest.

"Are you ready for this?" Paul mumbled close to her ear.

"About as ready as I'll ever be."

Servers floated in and out of the crowd carrying champagne glasses while others carried silver trays filled with elaborate hors d'oeuvres. The party was well on its way.

Someone approached them and took her wrap before Paul guided her farther into the house. They hadn't taken two steps before Martina spotted an older couple heading toward them. Martina knew immediately, that they were Paul's parents. She could see a little of him in each of them.

So this is Angelica Kendricks. Martina almost burst out laughing seeing her in an extravagant red evening gown, just like Jada predicted.

Dang that girl is good.

Paul's mother looked the way Martina expected. They were around the same height, but his mother appeared fit, she probably carried ten pounds more than Martina. Angelica's hair was swept up in an elaborate updo, showing off the diamonds dangling from her ears and around her neck. She had enough bling on to require a bodyguard. The woman looked like money.

Martina wasn't nervous, but when Paul placed his hand at the small of her back, she had to admit that it brought her a certain level of comfort.

She smiled up at him. She had a feeling he was more nervous than she. Was it because he thought she was going to embarrass him? Or maybe he thought that his mother wouldn't approve of her.

Martina wasn't one of those women concerned about what others thought of her, but she did care what Paul thought.

"Mother, Dad," Paul greeted.

Mother? He was such a laid back guy, hearing him refer to his mother in such a formal way as — *Mother*—seemed a bit stuffy.

Mrs. Kendricks leaned forward and turned her head slightly, giving Paul her cheek. Once he kissed her, Paul shook his father's hand.

"So who is this beautiful young lady?" His father's warm smile elicited one from her.

"This special lady is Martina Jenkins. Martina, these are my parents, Paul and Angelica Kendricks."

"Nice to meet you both." Martina extended her hand, but Angelica acted as if she didn't see it. Instead, she patted the back of her hair as she glanced behind her.

So it's like that, huh? No problem.

"It's a pleasure to meet you young lady." Paul's father accepted her hand, placing a kiss on the back of it. "Son, you are one lucky man."

"I couldn't agree more." He wrapped his arm around Martina, pulling her close then kissing her on the lips.

Martina didn't miss the way his mother's gaze started at the top of her head and didn't stop until it went down the length of her body and back up.

Martina smiled. She recognized the look. Jada had mastered it, a condescending admiration that masked her appreciation for the other woman's outfit.

"Oh, Paul, before I forget, I want you to say hello to Larry Kane. He and his wife can't stay long, so you should probably speak with him now." His mother slipped her arm through Paul's and started guiding him away.

"Mother, wait," he said and reached for Martina's hand.

"Dear, I'm sure Marcia can entertain herself for a few minutes without you."

"Her name is *Martina*," Paul corrected, irritation in his voice. "And I'm not going to leave her here. She goes where I go."

"Babe, that's all right. I'll be fine on my own. If I need you, I'll find you," Martina said pointedly, making sure to make eye contact with his mother.

When they strolled away, Paul's father said, "I'm sorry about my wife. She's determined to get Paul in front of the right people. People who can help him get into the White House."

Martina nodded, not trusting herself to say

anything.

"Can I get you something to drink?"

From behind her, a male voice said, "I can take care of that Uncle Paul while you see to your other guests."

Martina turned, surprised to see Davion.

"MJ, you're stunning. I almost didn't recognize you when you and Paul walked in. But then I know he wouldn't have been here with anyone else."

"Don't try to sweet-talk me after you tricked me into renovating Paul's house a few months ago."

He laughed and lifted his hands in surrender. "I'm sorry, but Paul's older and bigger than me. Besides, he threatened to tell my mother that I stole her pearls when we were ten. I just couldn't let that happen."

Martina laughed. "Whatever. You're lucky I kinda like you."

"How about I show you where the good food and drinks are since my aunt carted Paul off."

Martina glanced in the direction that Paul and his mother went. She saw him clear across the room standing with a man twice his age. Poor baby looked as if he would rather be on an exam table than listening to the guy.

As if he could sense her gaze locked on him, he glanced in her direction. She smiled and blew him a kiss. Her plan was to keep the peace and have a good time tonight. If that meant allowing his mother to drag him around like a little kid, she could deal with that.

"Shall we?" Davion offered his arm, and she allowed him to lead her away.

"So, where are you taking me?" Martina nodded a greeting to a few people who were looking at her as if they knew her. Since she didn't travel in the same circle and didn't recognize anyone, she kept moving.

"I'm going to introduce you to the second most important person in Paul's life."

"Who's the first?"

Davion narrowed his eyes at her. "You have to ask?"

Heat rushed to her cheeks. "Oh."

She wasn't sure who Davion was taking her to meet. It couldn't be Paul's sister Myra. He had told her that Myra couldn't attend because the baby was sick and her husband was on a business trip.

They strolled into the kitchen, of all places, where a flurry of activity was taking place. Once again, Martina was blown away at the size and exquisiteness of the space. Every appliance was supersized and top of the line. The light gray walls served as a backdrop for the dark custom cabinets and added extra warmth to the kitchen. A perfect choice. Like the rest of the home, no expense had been spared.

"Janice, I have someone here who you have to meet. This is Martina Jenkins, Paul's significant other. I'm sure if Aunt Angelica wasn't making him greet everyone in attendance, he would have introduced MJ."

Martina almost melted at the woman's warm smile.

"Oh, it is such a pleasure to finally meet you, sweetheart." She hugged Martina and it felt like being hugged by her grandmother. Katherine Jenkins gave the best hugs, but this woman definitely came in at a close second."

"Janice keeps this palace running like the White House," Davion said. "She's been with the family like…forever and practically raised Paul and his sisters."

That explained why Paul seemed to be from a different world than his mother. He had once told her that his parents traveled a lot when he was younger, leaving them with the housekeeper.

"It's nice to meet you too. Paul speaks highly of you. But what he talks about most are your Pecan Sandies."

Her smile made her face appear much younger. Janice was a beautiful woman and no doubt she turned a few heads in her youth. Her salt and pepper hair was pulled back into a tight bun at the nape of her neck. And her healthy, blemish-free face needed no makeup.

"It figures Paul would talk about food." Janice held Martina's hand, the smile never leaving her face. "You are as beautiful as I imagined."

"Thank you." No wonder Paul spoke about Janice more than his mother. This woman probably had more warmth in her pinky finger than Angelica had in her whole body.

"Are you hungry?" Janice asked. "Would you like to try some of the hors d'oeuvres that the other guests are having?" She leaned in close. "Or I can get you a plate of Chicken Marsala that I made especially for Paul and Davion."

Davion dropped his arm around Janice's shoulders. "Martina, take door number two. I assure you that you'll be licking your lips after tasting Janice's Chicken Marsala."

"Oh stop." Janice grinned and swatted at Davion.

"Actually if I can just have some water that would be fine for now." Martina seldom turned down food, but she was more thirsty than hungry.

Davion snatched a puff pastry off of a large tray that sat on the counter. Seeing all the food reminded Martina that she hadn't eaten anything since breakfast. Rarely did she miss a meal, but Jada had dragged her to get her hair and nails done, and then there was the makeup appointment. Before Martina realized it, the day had flown by.

A tingle scurried up Martina's back, and she didn't have to turn to know that Paul was nearby. When she glanced over her shoulder, her stomach did a flip-flop at the sight of him. He looked rich and powerful in his black, single-buttoned tuxedo. They'd only been apart for a few minutes, but his presence still had the ability to make her feel all gooey inside.

Now was no different. Dark intense eyes zoned in on her and the urge to run and leap into his arms was almost overwhelming. The last couple of months he had been an addiction she couldn't seem to break. She didn't want to break. All she wanted was to spend every waking hour with him and some days the thought scared her to death. But not tonight. Tonight her body was aware of him, longed for him and she intended to have her fill.

"Hey, baby. I'm sorry about abandoning you like that." He kissed her sweetly. "I see you've met Janice."

Martina shared a smile with Janice. "I have. She's been keeping me company. I was hanging with Davion, but as you can see, he abandoned me for food." She nodded her head toward his cousin who was eating at the kitchen table.

"Paul, I'll fix you a plate."

"That's okay, Janice." He kissed her on the cheek. "I just came in here to get my gorgeous date."

"Very well. You know where to find it when you're ready. I need to get back to work anyway." She hugged them both and scurried off.

Paul turned his attention to her, looking at her strangely.

"What?" Martina asked.

He lifted her chin with the pad of his finger, concern covering his face. "You feeling okay? You look a little flushed."

"Yeah, I feel fine. Maybe a little thirsty still." She held up the glass that she'd emptied. Or maybe warmth spreading through her body had more to do with taking in him and how hot he looked. Her internal temperature was probably through the roof. "Can you get me some more water?"

"Of course," he said, looking unconvinced.

When he came back with more water, she downed it as fast as before, setting the empty glass on a nearby counter.

"Thanks."

Paul reached for her hand and started toward the door. "Did you eat anything?"

"I'm not that hungry."

He stopped short. "Now I know something's wrong. You never turn down food. Are you sure you're feeling all right?"

She pulled on his hand. "Quit being a worry wart. I'm fine. Come on. Let's go and do a little meeting and greeting."

An hour later, Martina was more than ready to call it a night. She had never met so many boring people in all of her life. The scary part was, some of these people were friends of Paul. How he tolerated their company was a mystery to her. There were several times she had to hold her tongue for fear of sharing too much of her opinion.

"If I have to listen to Senator What's His Name, drone on and on in that Ben Stein monotone for another minute, I'm going to nail him in the butt with one of my too-tall-stilettos. Goodness!" Martina said when they eased away from the conversation with a couple of state senators and their wives.

Paul burst out laughing. "You held up better than I thought you would. I appreciate you doing this for me, baby." He kissed her lips.

"Don't thank me. I did it because I feel sorry for you. Like seriously, babe, how do you do it? I'm damn near comatose after less than an hour of listening to him while you've had to put up with his yammering for years."

Paul laughed so hard, tears filled his eyes. "You're crazy. I don't know how I've survived these parties without you by my side."

"I'm sorry you've had to." She leaned into him as they moved further away from the group, their arms around each other's waist. "Why don't I sit the next couple of minutes out and let you mingle. I think I'll hide out in the kitchen for a while."

"I'll come with you."

"Paul, I don't want your mother to get mad at me for dominating all of your attention." Martina had noticed Angelica glaring at her all evening.

"Don't worry about my mother. You're my number one priority." Paul pulled her off to the side into a secluded corner. "If you'd like, we can even sneak upstairs and test out my old bed."

Martina threw her head back and laughed. "I'm starting to rub off on you. That sounds more like something I would say."

"You can rub on me anytime, baby." She giggled when he nuzzled her neck and his hands did a slow glide down the side of her body. A sizzle of desire shot through her body to the tips of her toes and she knew she'd have to put a halt to his delicious assault before they got too carried away.

"Okay stop." She nudged him and glanced around to see if anyone could see them. "You have to get back in there. It's clear your mother had you in mind when she decided on her guest list. If I hear one more thing about a new Senate term or you being the next president, I think I'm going to scream."

He dropped his arms from around her and rubbed his forehead. "I know. I should have asked more questions about this party. If you want to leave, I—"

"Oh no, you don't. You're not going to use me as an excuse to cut out early." She dug through her small clutch and pulled out lipstick for a quick touch up. "I say go back in there, do what you do, and I'm going to hang out with Janice. I suddenly feel a little hungry."

She air-kissed him and hurried away before he could touch her again. A little bit more and she would've taken him up on his offer to see his old bedroom.

CHAPTER SEVENTEEN

Paul struggled to focus on what Senator Alfred Springs was saying as he spotted Martina the moment she stepped out of the kitchen. She roamed around the large great room, taking note of some of the art his parents had collected during their travels.

"My wife and I told your parents that we would be happy to host a fundraiser," Alfred said pulling Paul's attention back to the conversation. "I was glad to hear that you're planning…"

Again, Paul's gaze followed every move Martina made. A jab of possessiveness punched him in the gut. He wasn't the only one looking. There wasn't a man in the room, married or not, whose head didn't turn when she walked pass. But who could blame them? Any red-blooded man would be defenseless seeing her in that dress.

She turned slightly, giving him a good view of her beautiful face. How many times had he dreamed about this moment, where she would attend a function with him, and he could claim her as his woman? The last few months had given him hope that his plans for the future were attainable.

A closer look at Martina and he could see that she still appeared a little flushed.

"Oh and with the sta—"

"Alfred, I'm sorry, but please excuse me. I need to go and check on my date."

Paul walked away without giving the man a chance to say anything else. Half way to Martina his mother appeared out of nowhere and looped her arm through his.

"I need to talk to you." Yeah, and he needed to talk to her, but first, he wanted to make sure Martina was okay.

"Mother, this will have to wait. I need to check on Martina."

"This will only take a minute."

She led him to the back hall that connected the main house with the pool house. The stark white ceiling and flooring were such a contrast to everything else in the home. Windows lined each side of the hallway, bringing the outdoors inside.

"What is this I hear about you not planning to do another term in the Senate? And you have no intention of running for president?"

Paul looked at her as if she'd lost her mind. "I told you and Dad on more than one occasion that I'm done with politics. Clearly, neither of you have been listening."

"Nonsense," she waved her hand as if swatting a fly, "you can't be done with politics. This is who you are. Ever since your grandfather took you to the White House, you said you were going to be president."

"Mother, I was six. Plans and dreams change." He didn't bother mentioning his restaurant ideas. He'd be wasting his time. "I'm done living my life for you and dad. I should have gotten out of politics years ago." Instead, he lived an unfulfilled life in order to live up to the family's expectations. Those days were over.

His mother stood speechless as if she didn't understand what he was telling her.

"What will you do? No wait. It's that woman isn't it? I don't understand why you brought her to this party instead of escorting Antoinette. What were you thinking? She's not right for you and—"

"And you need to stop right there!" Paul seethed. "I let you get away with looking at her as if she was some second class citizen when we first arrived, because I didn't want to make a scene. But you need to understand. That woman that you're badmouthing is the woman I plan to marry one day. So if you can't show her some respect, not only will you not have to worry about her coming back, but you'll never see me again either."

"Paul Kendricks Jr.!" She narrowed her eyes. "I don't know what has gotten into you, but I will not tolerate you speaking to me like that! I'm sorry if I offended that woman, but she's classless, this is an all-black affair, and the hussy wore red."

He gave a humorless laugh. "What's the big deal? You have on red."

"But dear, I'm the hostess and besides that's not the point. I want you to stop telling people that you're done with politics. The last thing I need is for the media to catch wind of this before I have a chance to change—"

"Stop." Paul shook his head. Why was he even

bothering? "I originally planned to announce to your entire group in there my political plans—"

"You will do no such thing! I will not have you embarrass your father and I this evening with this nonsense. You will not sully the Kendricks family legacy."

"Fine. They can find out like everyone else at my press conference." He turned to walk away, but stopped when she grabbed hold of the back of his tuxedo jacket.

"Paul ... let's calm down. I didn't call you out here to upset you. I don't want us arguing tonight. Why don't we go back to the party and try to enjoy the rest of the evening?"

His mother held onto his arm as they strolled back inside.

"Oh, did you get a chance to speak to Antoinette this evening? You must say hello. She looks absolutely stunning and appropriate in her *black* evening gown."

Paul shook his head and sighed.

I quit.

*

Martina stood in front of the bathroom mirror and dabbed at the perspiration on her forehead. She'd felt warm all night. At first she assumed the heat in the home was up high. Now she wondered if she was coming down with something.

They had been at the party a couple of hours, more than enough time for Paul to mingle with the guest. A few minutes ago, she had seen him heading in her direction, but he'd been intercepted by three older gentlemen. She waited, hoping the conversation would be quick, but no such luck. Whatever they were discussing seemed as if it would take a while.

Martina rinsed her hands in the sink, finally ready to head home and get out of those ridiculous heels. Her cousin, Jada could walk all day in the mall in heels twice as high all for the sake of looking cute. Admittedly, the shoes were cute, but after a couple hours, it was time to get out of them. They were killing her feet.

She quickly dried her hands and exited the bathroom. Paul's mother glided toward her.

Oh great. The last person I want to see.

All night the woman had been looking at her as if she were a piece of gum stuck on the bottom of her Louboutins.

So far Angelica hadn't said much to Martina. Really, she hadn't said anything. It was the various glares she'd lobbed across the room that said she didn't want Martina there.

"Did my son mention to you that this was an all-black party - meaning everyone was to wear black?"

"Yes he did," Martina answered. She let her gaze slide over Paul's mother before making eye contact again. "But like you, I march to my own beat."

Mrs. Kendricks gasped, her hand covering her chest and eyes blinking rapidly in shock.

Martina wanted to laugh at her dramatic reaction but held back.

"I'm familiar with your grandparents," Angelica huffed. "Surely they don't condone this type of behavior."

Oh, crap. Why'd she have to mention them?

"No they don't," Martina finally said, feeling duly chastised. She should have kept her previous response short and sweet, but no, she had to go there. Being tired and finally a little hungry wasn't helping.

"Well, I don't tolerate that type of behavior either. As a matter of fact, I should insist you leave."

Anger swelled inside of Martina and her hands fisted at her sides. She ground her teeth together, fighting to keep her mouth closed, but knowing it was a losing battle.

Her grandmother's speech about respect swirled inside of her head. Martina hesitated before speaking, trying to choose her words carefully.

"Forgive me, Mrs. Kendricks if you feel that I've disrespected you. But you've been giving me the side-eye since I walked through those double doors, but that's okay. I honestly don't care what you think of me though there's something you should know. I love your son. He is an incredible man and the best thing that has ever happened to me. So we can either try to get along for his sake…or not. It's your choice, but right now, I'm not doing this with you. I'm going to find my man."

Martina turned too quick on her too-high heels and stumbled, but quickly righted herself with the help of the wall.

Shoulders back, head up, Jada had coached. *Walk like you own the place.*

Feeling the daggers through her back from Paul's mother's gaze, Martina kept it moving. It was time for her and Paul to make their exit, before she forgot all of her home training.

CHAPTER EIGHTEEN

Three days after the Kendrick's party, Martina sat in her mother's kitchen, finally ready to make amends. She had put the conversation off long enough. Dealing with Angelica Kendricks made her realize that the problem between her and her mother could be fixed. As for Paul and his mother, Martina wasn't so sure.

Her heart went out to him. On their way home from the party, he had told her about the conversation with Angelica. Martina felt his disappointment in his mother deep in her soul, but had no idea what to say to him. All she could do going forward was to support his decisions and his dream of opening a restaurant.

"Are you sure I can't get you something else?" Martina's mother asked when she walked back into the kitchen. "Soup, maybe?"

"No, the ginger ale is good. I guess my two chili dogs, onion rings and the macaroni salad I had for lunch today didn't mix well. And Blaine's girlfriend brought some cute little pecan pies out to the job site during our afternoon break. Oh, my goodness, they were incredible. I think I had three too many. Now that I think about it, that combination of food in one day, probably wasn't a good idea."

Her mother laughed and a warm feeling flowed through Martina, glad she could put the smile on Carolyn's face. How many times had they argued about one thing or another? The mother daughter relationship had gotten so bad at times that the family tried keeping them apart, especially during Sunday brunch.

"Sometimes you scare me in how much alike we are. Your lunch sounds almost identical to mine, except I had two regular hot dogs, garlic fries and a humongous chunk of sweet potato pie."

Their healthy appetite and cast iron stomach was definitely something they had in common. Martina inherited her mother's metabolism as well. Carolyn was a perfect size six despite the way she put away food.

"Hopefully, your stomach is handling your meal better than mine," Martina said, rubbing her belly as if that would ease some of the nausea. "It feels as if there's a tidal wave crashing inside of me tossing my organs around."

They shared another laugh then sat in silence until Carolyn spoke.

"I guess your grandmother was right. We are a lot alike." Carolyn sat in the chair across from Martina. "By the way, you weren't the only one who received a speech from Momma. The day after she talked to you, she gave me an ear full."

"Tell me your talk wasn't as painfully honest as the

one she gave me."

"Oh but it was. It was probably worse. However, I needed to hear everything she had to say."

"Mom, I'm sorry for my jacked-up attitude all of these years. I know an apology this late in the game isn't much, but I really am sorry. I shouldn't have taken my frustrations out on you. Nor should I have disrespected you the way that I did."

"I deserved it, MJ," Carolyn said without hesitation. "I should have been straight with you from day one about your father, about everything. If you want to meet him, I can—"

"I don't. He's dead to me," Martina said without emotion. What little she knew about the man, she didn't like. Her grandparents were good judges of character and if they hadn't seen fit for her to get to know him from day one, she trusted their decision. Besides, meeting him now wouldn't benefit anyone as far as she was concerned.

"Okay," her mother said slowly, as if waiting to see if Martina was going to say more. When Martina didn't, she continued. "I also should've tried harder to connect with you, but I was too ashamed. I made so many mistakes on so many different levels over the years. You had every right to feel the way you did about me, especially since I didn't try harder to be a good mother."

"And I know I didn't make it easy."

Martina had made her share of mistakes as an adult and hadn't considered that her mother was just a woman, trying to figure life out like everyone else. It was so easy to put her in a certain category and expect her to behave the way Martina thought a mother should behave. But she shouldn't have judged her, especially since she hadn't known what all her mother had gone through.

"I'm sure we could go back and forth on who's the one most at fault for our broken relationship. Why don't we call it even?" Carolyn said.

"Works for me."

Her mother lifted a finger. "I have one condition."

Martina laughed remembering a conversation with Paul. "In the words of my man, I'm not negotiating for love. We either hug, and make up, or we don't." They both laughed, and Carolyn pulled Martina up and into her arms.

"I love you, baby." She placed a kiss against her hair.

Martina held on tight. She couldn't remember the last time she'd allowed her mother to hug her. It felt good. Real good.

"I love you too, Mom."

"Speaking of your *man*. Tell me about him. Do you think he's the one?"

They talked and laughed, comparing dating horror stories. Martina knew they would never get back the years they had lost, but she had every intention of making the rest of the years the best she could make them.

*

When his doorbell rang, Paul turned down the heat under the bacon and went to the door, Charlie hot on his heels.

"Sit." Paul pointed to the floor just inside the front door. For the past few weeks, Charlie had spent more time with his sister and her family than he had with Paul. His nieces wanted to keep him all the time, but Paul was thinking about getting them a puppy of their own for Christmas.

Paul opened the door for Davion, who walked in with a carton of orange juice.

"This is my contribution to breakfast this fine Sunday morning." He shook out of his coat and tossed it on a nearby chair before ruffling Charlie's fur. "What's up, boy? I haven't seen you for a while."

"Come on back. I'm in the kitchen."

Davion made a beeline for the half bathroom to wash his hands, and when he stepped into the kitchen, he said, "I'm not interrupting breakfast with you and your baby by not calling first am I?"

"Fine time to ask. You're here now." Paul turned the bacon. Since being back together, Martina had been spending most of her days at his place, whether he was in town or not. He loved having her around.

"I'm glad you stopped by. I might have gotten a little carried away with breakfast." Paul had cooked as if he were expecting a basketball team.

"Oh good, you made chocolate chip pancakes. I was hoping for more than just hash browns, bacon, and eggs."

"For a person who can't cook a lick, you sure are demanding." Paul pulled down plates, glasses, and a couple of coffee mugs. "Dig in."

"So where's MJ?"

"She's at her house meeting with a realtor." Paul told him about how Martina flips houses. She never ceased to impress him. If he wasn't mistaken, this was the third house she'd done in five years with a desire to do more.

"So her selling her home might feed right into your plans of making an honest woman out of her. When are you going to pop the question?"

"Soon." Paul had no doubt that she was the woman for him, but Martina was still a little skittish. He knew she loved him. She was all in as far as them going public with their relationship, but he had to tread lightly when it came to the subject of marriage.

"Is Aunt Angelica still giving you the silent treatment?"

"Yep. Three weeks and she acts as if I stole one of her fur coats. Myra had me drop the kids off over there a couple of days ago, and I figured that my mother and I could talk through our differences. Wrong. All of her attention was on the kids, and she pretended as if I weren't there."

Davion chuckled. "Unbelievable. She acts as if the sun rises and sets on her grandchildren, but with you and your sisters, it's another story."

"I know, right? I can't ever remember her or my father spending that much time with us. Granted, they were trying to build their legacy, according to my father, but it was at the sacrifice of building a relationship with us. I'm sure that has something to do with why Kacy only comes to town once or twice a year." His sister and her family lived in Los Angeles and usually only visited Ohio in the summer, if then.

"I'm still shocked your mom and MJ had words. Then again, neither one of them could ever be accused of keeping their thoughts to themselves." Davion laughed. "I just wished I'd been there."

"Yeah, me too." Paul wished he had been there for other reasons. Martina didn't tell him about her encounter with his mother until they had left the Kendricks' estate. Paul wanted to turn back around, but Martina insisted that it had been handled. She warned him that there might be some backlash, but he wasn't concerned with the repercussions. He hated that she had to deal with his mother alone. He should have kept Martina close, protected her from his mother. However, knowing Martina, his mother might have been the one who needed shielding.

A smile spread across his lips. Martina was a fighter. Not so much physically, but her words could cut a person down with little or no effort on her part. He had been on the receiving end of her verbal beat-downs on more than one occasion.

Yep, she is definitely more than capable of fighting her battles.

CHAPTER NINETEEN

A week later, Martina paced the length of her master bathroom, stopping periodically to glance at the small, unopened box on the bathroom vanity. The sight of it produced the same type of fear that a gray-eyed serpent, with a long, slimy tongue would elicit.

She stopped in front of the sink and swallowed. Her pulse pounded like the bass in a Parliament Funkadelic song on steroids, and she could barely catch her breath.

She pressed her hand against her chest as if that could stop her heart from beating so fast.

God, please don't let me be having a heart attack. And please don't let me be pregnant.

I can't be pregnant.

You wouldn't do this to me...

The doorbell rang, and she debated on whether or not to answer. She was in no condition to have company, not even if it was one of her cousins ... especially if it was one of her cousins. Then again, maybe she needed them. One of them. Not all of them. Her nerves were too fragile.

The doorbell rang again.

Seconds later she swung the door open, surprised to see Paul standing there with a pizza box.

"What are you doing here?" she asked, but the scent of onions, basil and tomatoes permeated the air and sent her racing to the bathroom. She barely made it to the toilet before her stomach lurched, emptying its contents.

"Hey. You okay?" Paul asked when he entered the bathroom moments after her.

Too exhausted to answer, she wiped her mouth with the back of her hand and slumped against the wall. She watched from the floor as he lifted the home pregnancy box from the vanity and slowly turned to her.

Oh damn. Why couldn't it have been Peyton? Toni? Heck, she would have even taken Jada.

Martina assumed she must have looked pretty bad. Instead of asking the burning question, he flushed the toilet and quickly grabbed a washcloth from the linen cabinet. His calm demeanor was unnerving. Why did he have to be so in control? It might have been better if he were yelling.

Of course, he wasn't the yelling type. Maybe that was good, especially since she was. Another reason he was the perfect man for her.

Paul wet the washcloth and then proceeded to wipe her face and hands as if she were a child. Hell, at the moment, she felt like a child. What the heck was she going to do with a kid? That's assuming she was pregnant.

God, please don't let me be pregnant.

Concern showed on Paul's handsome face as he

continued tending to her.

"What are you doing here?" she asked again. "I thought you were going to be in D. C. this weekend."

"I was, but you didn't sound too good when I talked to you last night, and I was worried. Looks like it's a good thing I came home."

He helped her stand, hovering as she brushed her teeth and rinsed her mouth.

"How long have you been like this?"

"Like what? Feeling like crap or hanging out in this stupid bathroom?"

"How long have you been feeling like crap?"

"Off and on for a couple of weeks," she said just above a whisper, her stomach feeling nauseous. "Maybe a little longer. I'm not sure."

Her gaze met his in the mirror, and she waited for the onslaught of questions. Not that she could answer any of them since she wasn't sure if she was even pregnant.

"Why didn't you tell me?"

"Tell you what, Paul? That I screwed up and might be pregnant," she spat, wanting to hate him, but was secretly glad he was there.

"Yeah, that might've worked. At least I would have been here for you." He turned her to face him. "You've been sick all this time and haven't said anything." He pushed curls away from her face and rested his hand on her cheek. "Don't you know how important you are to me? And you might be carrying my child."

Yes, she knew how important she was to him. He showed her whether he was in town or not. The man was truly an angel, always looking out for her. When her truck died a few days ago, within a couple of hours, a brand new truck had been delivered.

It's an early Christmas present, he had told her.

Her feelings for him grew stronger and stronger every day they were together, but she wasn't ready to be his baby's momma.

God, please don't let me be pregnant. I can't be pregnant.

She dropped her head to Paul's hard chest, trying to calm her withering nerves.

"I guess I should go ahead and take the test. No need to keep us both in suspense," she said dryly and grabbed the box.

Paul leaned against the sink and crossed his arms and then his ankles as if hanging out in a small bathroom was the most natural thing in the world to do.

She looked at him pointedly. "Surely you don't think I'm going to pee in front of you."

He dropped his arms and stood upright. "You're kidding, right? Baby, I have seen everything you have." He eased up to her, his hand on her waist as he lowered his lips to her neck. "And I've tasted every inch of your enticing body. I even—"

"Might've gotten me pregnant!" She pushed against his shoulder. "So don't touch me! Get out!"

His laughter followed him out of the bathroom.

Minutes later Martina sat on the side of the tub shocked as she stared at the little white stick that showed two fuchsia-colored lines.

Pregnant.

How did this happen? No. She knew, exactly how it happened and was pretty sure she could pinpoint when. What she couldn't believe is that after being raised by a single mother, with no plans to ever marry and have children, she was pregnant.

God, I can't be pregnant, she groaned and dropped her head into her hands.

Despair lodged in her throat and tears pricked the back of her eyes. All these years she had judged her mother, and here she was in the same predicament. Sure maybe she wasn't as young as her mother had been, and Martina did have a good job, but still...

"Martina? Baby, you okay in there?"

Oh God, I can't be pregnant.

*

Paul knocked again on the bathroom door, worry bouncing around inside of him. When Martina still didn't answer, he eased the door open.

From the doorway, his gaze found her huddled in the corner near the tub. His heart lurched. The vulnerability he saw in her eyes stabbed him in the chest. She didn't have to say a word. Her forlorn expression said it all.

Without speaking, he scooped her into his arms and held her tight, placing a kiss against her temple. He carried her into the bedroom, concerned that she still hadn't spoken. He had expected her to at least curse him out.

Paul never thought he would want to hear her yelling at him, but right now, he would give anything to hear her fussing. About anything.

She said nothing. No words. No tears. Nothing.

Instead, she clung to him as if he were a lifeline.

Paul didn't know how long he stood near the bed just holding Martina. Eventually, he laid her down and climbed in next to her.

They laid in silence for what seemed like hours but were probably only a few minutes. He had no idea what she was thinking. Sure he was in love with her and ready for marriage, but this route wasn't what he had in mind.

The silence gave him time to think. Suddenly he smiled in the dimness of the room. A thrill of excitement shot through his body.

We're having a baby. I'm going to be a father!

The thought swirled around in his head as his excitement grew. He had waited a long time for this moment, but it had played out very different in his dreams. He imagined he'd be married to Martina of course, but would wait a year before having children.

Martina stirred next to him, and he pulled her closer, her butt against the front of his body. He placed a kiss near her ear.

They had a lot to talk about, but for now, he was okay with just holding the mother of his unborn child.

Martina turned to face him. "What am I going to do? I can't have a baby."

Paul stiffened. His pulse ratcheted up as he thought about the meaning behind her words.

No. No way would she…

He didn't bother finishing the thought. Paul didn't even want to think about the alternative, and he knew her well enough to know that she wasn't thinking about getting rid of their baby. At least, he hoped he knew her, but the worried look on her face sent his pulse racing.

Martina must have sensed his anxiousness. Her brows dipped into a frown while she studied him as if trying to read his mind.

"Say something."

He let the back of his hand glide slowly down the side of her face. Her skin, flawless and soft, had him wanting to touch her all the time.

"I'm not sure what to say. When you said you couldn't have this baby, I—"

"I might be scared shitless, but I would *never* terminate a pregnancy if that's what you're thinking."

The conviction in her voice helped settle him down, and Paul didn't think his love for her could grow even stronger than it already was.

"Are you sure the test is correct? We always used protection. So I don't know how this—"

"Not always. We didn't use protection every single time."

He tilted his head slightly trying to remember a time when they hadn't used a condom. His memory suddenly took him back to that first night there at her place. Realization dawned on him recalling their second round of lovemaking.

By the look in her eyes, he didn't have to say anything. They were both remembering that night. They'd always been combustible sexually, but that night their lovemaking had gone to a whole different level.

Martina flipped onto her back, her forearm across her eyes.

"How did I let this happen?"

"First of all, *you* didn't let this happen." Paul slid closer, his thigh rubbing against her bare legs. He laid his hand on her stomach still trying to picture her being pregnant and him being a father. "It took both of us. Together we'll figure out our next steps."

He knew what he wanted to do. He was crazy in love with her and had wanted to marry her since the first time he'd seen her walk into the coffee shop in her steel toe boots. Add a baby to the equation and he was floating on cloud nine. Convincing Martina that getting married was the best solution for them wasn't going to be easy. As a matter of fact, he might have to have a few glasses of liquid courage to prepare himself for the verbal battle he knew was coming.

"I think the first thing we need to do is get you to a doctor."

She released a frustrated sigh. "Yeah, I'll call Monday for an appointment."

"Well, let me know the day and time so I can go with you."

She lifted her arm slightly and met his gaze. "That won't be necessary. Paul, I don't expect you to stop everything you have going on to accompany me to every appointment. That's just not realistic. Besides, it'll cost an arm and a leg for you to travel back and forth like that."

Sometimes he thought she forgot that he had money. As a matter of fact, he had more money than he could spend in a lifetime. Getting to and from Cincinnati within a couple of hours wasn't a problem. His problem was getting it through her thick skull that he wanted to be a part of every aspect of her life, even more if that test she had just taken was correct.

Paul placed a finger under her chin, forcing her to drop her arm and look at him.

"Let me explain something to you. I know you don't want to hear this because you're ridiculously stubborn, but I love you. Martina Jenkins, I have loved you from the first day we met and despite the time we were a part, that hasn't changed."

She shook her head and tried moving away, but he held her in place.

"I know. Sometimes I don't know why you put up

with me. Why you love me." Tears filled her eyes, but she didn't let them fall. "You are an amazing, good-looking man who can have any woman you want. Why me?"

Clearly these were hormones talking, Paul thought.

"Why not you? You're fun, intelligent, absolutely stunning and give me hell about everything. What's not to love? You're perfect for me."

She grunted and shook her head.

"Well, I hope you know you're going to have to be a stay at home dad because I'm not quitting my job."

Paul threw his head back and burst out laughing. Her quick wit and smart mouth were only a couple of reasons why he was madly and passionately in love with this woman.

CHAPTER TWENTY

The Friday after her doctor's appointment, confirming that she was indeed pregnant, Martina walked into the bar and grill where she was meeting her cousins. She and Paul debated on when they would start telling people, but Martina knew she wouldn't be able to keep something like this from the girls.

She walked over to their usual booth and slid in next to Peyton.

"It's about time you got here," Toni said from across the table, sitting next to Jada. "Why is it that you and CJ are always the last to arrive?"

"Why is it that you have to be a mother hen and monitor who comes early or late?"

"Apparently, Paul isn't putting it on her as well as I thought he was capable of," Jada said and sipped from her wine glass, "because if he were, maybe she would have a better disposition."

Before she could blurt out the smart remark begging to be released, Sue, the server, came to the table.

"The usual for you, MJ? Double cheeseburger, smothered fries, onion rings and a beer?"

Just hearing Sue rattle off her usual order made Martina queasy.

"No. I'll have a cheeseburger and some water." Martina didn't have to look around the table to know they all were staring at her, even Sue. She hadn't ordered that small of a meal in all of her adult life.

But before any of them could speak, Christina rushed in grinning like she had just won a billion dollars.

"Guess what? I'm engaged!" she screamed, waving her hand in their faces.

Martina's head volleyed back and forth, as everyone talked at once. She was super happy for Christina and knew months ago that it was only a matter of time before Luke proposed.

"He said he was going to wait until next week and propose on Christmas, but I'm glad he didn't. I had a feeling he was up to something."

"Oh my God, CJ," Jada pulled on Christina's hand, holding it still. "This looks like it's from the Ritani Endless Love Collection, and it's at least five-carats." Jada went on and on about the uniqueness of the engagement ring.

Good Lord. This girl is a walking encyclopedia for anything fashion and expensive.

They talked and laughed for the next few minutes, wedding ideas flowed around the table.

Peyton bumped Martina in the shoulder. "You okay?" she whispered.

"I'm fine…just pregnant."

It was as if time stood still and all eyes at the table

were on her. Martina hadn't realized she said it loud enough for everyone to hear.

"What?"

"Are you serious?"

"How?"

They all lobbed question after question at her, and Martina didn't know who was asking what.

She lifted her hands. "Stop! First of all, congrats, cuz. I think you and the thug lawyer are perfect for each other."

"Martina, quit stalling and start talking!" Toni ground out. "And start at the beginning."

Martina didn't know where to start and said the first thing that came to mind. "In the beginning, God created—"

"So help me if you don't quit playin' and start talking, we are going to hurt you." Christina pounded on the table and slid into the booth beside Martina. "Talk!"

Martina leaned away from Christina and gasped. "You would hurt a pregnant woman? So much for your tree-hugging, save the bees and whales act."

Martina laughed at the threatening look on each of their faces. She hadn't given them a hard time in a while. Why not make up for lost time?

"Sometimes I can't stand you," Christina grumbled.

Peyton bumped Martina's leg. "Stop messing around and tell us."

Martina gave them the highlights as they ate, glad to have someone to talk to other than Paul. He was super excited about the baby, and if she were honest with herself, she was getting there. Even at eight weeks, some moments being pregnant still didn't feel real. Needless to say, she and Paul were surprised to learn how far along she was. She hadn't known she was pregnant sooner because she had gotten her period, though very light, during the first four weeks. After a thorough examination, the doctor confirmed she and the baby were fine.

"We could have a double wedding," Christina said excitedly. "We're thinking a destination wedding in Fe—"

"In everything I just told you, did you once hear me say anything about getting married?" Martina shook her head and snatched one of Peyton's fries. "Just because Paul and I are having a baby, doesn't mean we have to get married."

Martina needed to make sure Paul understood that too before he started getting any ideas.

*

A week after Christmas Martina pulled into the garage surprised to see Paul's SUV. He had flown to California, to see his sister for a couple of days, but wasn't expected back for another day.

The moment she walked into the house, the smell of roasted peppers and onions drew her in like a bee to honey. Her mouth watered and her stomach chose that moment to rumble. Her appetite had returned with a vengeance and by the glorious aromas filling the house, she was glad it had.

"Paul?" she called out when she didn't find him in the kitchen. She also realized right away that she didn't hear Charlie. "Where are you?"

"I'm in here."

She made it to the dining room and paused in the doorway. She knew he had skills in the kitchen, but this was the first time that he had gone to the trouble of creating a romantic atmosphere.

The lights were slightly dimmed and tall, tapered candles graced the center of the table.

"What's all this?"

Paul walked toward her and handed her a single red rose before pulling her into his arms.

"This is because I've missed you. I'm realizing that any day away from you is too long."

He lowered his head, and the softness of his lips had her forgetting about everything. From the exhausting day at work, to the traffic she had been sitting in for the past half an hour. Nothing mattered but that moment. She fell in love with him more and more every day.

Martina was so glad to see him, so happy to be in his arms. He had asked her to travel with him, but she and her crew were trying to finish a job before the New Year, and they were behind schedule.

"How was your day?" he asked when he lifted his head, but kept a hand on her hip.

"Better now. Much better." She pulled out of his hold and moved closer to the decorative table where several covered dishes and fine china was laid out. "So what's the occasion?"

"Well, a couple of weeks ago I found out the woman I'm madly in love with is having my baby." He pulled out Martina's chair.

"Well that woman you're referring to had better be me or things are going to get real ugly, real fast. I'm just sayin'."

He shook his head and laughed. "You're the only woman for me, *and* you're the only one who's having my baby. As a matter of fact, you're the only woman I could ever imagine being the mother of my child." He sat at the head of the table to her right.

Martina hadn't noticed the bottle of sparkling apple juice until Paul picked up one of the champagne flutes and filled it.

He handed her a glass, and he lifted his for a toast.

"Here's to us and a healthy baby."

They tapped glasses, and both took a sip.

Martina noticed Paul was having the same.

"Just because I can't drink alcohol, doesn't mean you can't."

"I'm good. I figured if you have to give up alcohol for the next few months, I can too."

Martina smiled behind the rim of her glass. "What else are you planning to give up over the next few months? Are you planning to read every book that I'm going to have to read, go to Lamaze class at some point, and take up prenatal yoga?"

Paul shrugged. "Yep." Now he was the one smiling at her surprised expression. "I'm in this one-hundred percent, baby."

"I see."

Conversation flowed easily, as they feasted on grilled salmon. Paul told her about his trip and plans for the next few weeks before he had to return to D.C. When he mentioned the Senate having to vote on a few bills, she couldn't help but think about the situation with the unions. Instead of bringing up the volatile topic and risk ruining the evening, she just listened. A first for her.

"As usual, dinner was delicious. Thank you for cooking. I had planned to pull out the leftover pot roast I made yesterday." She stood, prepared to clear the table until he stopped her with a hand on her arm.

"I'll take care of the cleanup. Have a seat." He

nodded toward her vacated chair. "There's something I want to ask you."

"What is it?"

He held her hand as he slowly knelt on one knee next to her chair.

She swallowed hard. When he pulled out a small velvet box, Martina was glad she was sitting.

"Since the day I met you, I've thought about what it would be like to have you as my wife. For a while, all I could imagine was more of our heated discussions and you challenging me at every turn. Then the better I got to know you, thoughts of spending my life with you filled my mind almost constantly."

"Oh, Paul…" Martina's hand went to her mouth.

"Baby you're everything I've ever wanted in a wife. You're witty, crazy smart, compassionate, hard-working, an excellent cook and I could go on and on. I love you more than I ever thought I could ever love another human being. And now that you're pregnant with our baby, I couldn't think of a better time to ask you this. Martina Jenkins, would you do me the honor of being my wife?"

He held the platinum ring, with a modest diamond in the center and smaller diamonds on the sides, between his fingers.

Martina's heart pounded like a freight train roaring down the tracks.

"If you don't like it, just say the word, and I'll get you another one. I knew you wouldn't want anything big and pretentious, but—"

"It's beautiful," she said quietly, afraid to reach for the impressive piece. All she could do was stare. Knowing Paul, he had probably paid a small fortune for the ring since he had no qualms about spending money. She also knew he was waiting for an answer.

"As I got older," Martina started, "I vowed that I would never be like my mother. I had no intention of having a child, especially out of wedlock. But Paul, I can't marry you just because I'm pregnant. I appreciate you asking me, but—."

"Martina." He pulled his chair closer and sat. "I'm not asking you because you're pregnant. I'm asking you because I love you. I want to spend the rest of my life with you. Honey, I know getting pregnant is not something either of us planned, but I'm not sorry. I want this baby more than I can express, but even more, I want you to be my wife. I want you to move in with me, make this house a home and for us to live happily-ever-after together. That's what I want. What do you want?"

Martina stared into his eyes and the love she felt for him exploded inside of her chest. She had already taken a chance on admitting her love for him. Maybe now it was time to take the biggest leap of her life.

"Tell me what you want," he repeated.

"Besides wanting a big chunk of the chocolate cake I saw on the kitchen counter, I want to be your wife. I love you, Paul. I love you so frickin much it scares the hell out of me."

He leaped out of his chair and pulled her into his arms, hugging her to his hard body. The love and warmth she felt in his arms was enough to ease some of her fears and anxiety.

Paul slowly released her and then reached for her hand.

"You know, I don't need a ring."

He met her gaze and maintained the hold on her

hand.

"I know there is nothing traditional about you." He smiled, making her insides melt. "You might not need a ring, but *I* need you to have one." He slid it onto her finger. "This symbolizes that we exclusively belong to each other. I'm in this forever, baby. And I promise you that I will do everything in my power to make you happy."

She cupped his cheek and smiled. "I know you will, and I'm already happy. But so that you know, if you hurt me, I'm going to hunt you down with my nail gun and…"

His mouth covered hers with the sweetest kiss he'd ever given her, halting all conversation. It was as if he was transmitting every ounce of love he felt for her, through his lips almost bringing her to tears.

Martina didn't know what the future held, but if she was going to journey to parts unknown, this was the man she wanted by her side. A deep feeling of peace consumed her, and she felt ready for the next chapter of her life. She couldn't believe she was about to get married and have a baby. Steps she never expected to take, but she was determined to embrace the changes.

When the kiss ended, she cupped his jaw and stared into his eyes smiling. "Okay, so I have a couple of conditions."

He pulled away and laughed. "Yeah, I'm sure you do, but so that you know, I'm going to treat you like the remarkable woman you are. We are going to have an unbelievable life together. Now come on. Let's get that cake. I have to make sure I keep my pregnant, soon-to-be-wife happy."

*

Paul returned to the dining room with a glass of milk, and an extra pep in his step that Martina accepted his proposal without much pushback. He'd been prepared to wear her down with all of the reasons why they were perfect for each other and should get married. Fortunately, he didn't have to do much convincing. He wasn't sure if that was a good thing, or if he should be concerned. Very concerned.

Martina cut into the slice of cake and moaned. Paul loved that she enjoyed a good meal and those few weeks when she wasn't eating concerned him more than he let on. Now that her appetite had returned, he planned to keep her fed with all of her favorite dishes.

"You need to add this to the menu when you open your restaurant."

"I'll do that. Maybe I'll have an area on the menu labeled - Martina's Favorites."

She glanced at him. He didn't ever think he'd get tired of seeing that smile and those dazzling eyes. Marrying her and having a baby were additional reasons for not accepting another term in the Senate.

"What do you think about us getting married right away?" Paul asked between bites. Again, he braced himself for some push back. He had always thought that whenever he married, he and his bride-to-be would have a huge wedding surrounded by family and friends. But he would be totally fine with going to the courthouse or even flying to Vegas.

"How soon?"

The question was spoken so quietly that he hadn't been sure if she'd said anything until she met his gaze.

"I was thinking within the next month. I know it won't be easy to pull a big wedding together on—"

"I don't need, nor do I want a big wedding."

Paul studied her for a moment. Though she said yes to his proposal, he needed to make it clear that she had a choice on when they got married and how big of a wedding she wanted.

"Listen, babe. You already know how long I've wanted to make you my wife, but if you're not ready. Just tell me. As long as I have you in my life, that's what's most important to me."

She lifted the glass of milk to her lips and took a gulp before setting the glass back down.

"And you know me well enough to know that I don't do anything I don't want to do. I want this. I want to be your wife, and since I'm pregnant, I think it's a good idea we get married as soon as possible."

He wrapped his arm around her shoulder and pulled her close, kissing the top of her head.

"What type of wedding do you want?" he asked, his arm resting on the back of her chair. "Are we talking, big, small or what?"

She sat back in her seat and his fingers automatically went to her shiny curls while he waited for her to respond.

"I assume you probably know a judge or two."

Paul's hand stilled in her hair. "Yeah, I know a few," he responded carefully, hoping the conversation would go in the direction he wanted it to. He'd marry her right then and there if he could, but with her huge family, he assumed she would want everyone in attendance.

"Do you know one well enough to talk into coming here next Saturday morning?"

His eyebrows shot up. "You want to get married here … at the house? Next Saturday?"

"Yes. You said we could do whatever I want. That's what I want. Is that a problem?"

He sat forward. "Not a problem for me. I'm just surprised you're willing to get married that soon *and* that you want to get married here. This place is big, but the way you talk about the Jenkins clan, I wonder if there's enough room inside for everyone we invite. And it's too cold to get married outside."

"I just want it to be us and maybe a witness, or two. But that's it." She turned in her seat and reached for his hand, caressing the top of it with her thumb. "Paul, I never planned to get married. Never. So a wedding and all the bells and whistles were never a part of any fantasy that I had. I don't need a big wedding."

"What about your family? I know how important they are to you. Are you sure you don't want them to be a part of this?" There were easily forty people at the brunch he attended, and everyone seemed really close. Paul couldn't understand why she wouldn't want all of her family in attendance.

Martina sighed and released his hand. "Some will be disappointed, like my cousins. And some will be downright pissed, like my grandparents, especially my grandmother. She had a few not so pleasant words for Jada after she eloped. Although, they might not be too broken up since none of them expect me to ever get married."

"What about *you*? Are you going to be disappointed if we don't have a big wedding? I know I suggested we get married in a few weeks, but I have no problem waiting so we can plan a bigger wedding if that's what you want."

Martina shook her head. "I don't want the stress

of a big wedding. I remember when Peyton got married years ago. The plans started small and within a heartbeat, the wedding was twice the size she originally planned thanks to my grandmother and aunts. My family would mean well, but I don't want to go through that. I love you, Paul. If we're going to do this, I want our wedding to be about just you and me. Not everyone else."

She stood and paced near the table. The last thing Paul wanted was for her to have any regrets, but he had to trust that she was making the right decision for her. He knew his mother was going to have a fit if he got married without her and everyone she knew in attendance, but he didn't care. Right now, all he cared about was keeping Martina happy.

Paul stopped her from moving with a hand on her wrist. "What else are you thinking?"

"I want it to be you, me, a judge, and two witnesses."

"Oookay. Do you have two people in mind?"

"Yes. Peyton and Davion."

Paul nodded. "I know I can get Davion here, but what about Peyton?"

"Once she gets over the shock, she'll be here. But just in case, don't call the judge yet."

CHAPTER TWENTY-ONE

Martina paced in front of Peyton's desk, stopping every few minutes, glancing at the ring Paul had placed on her finger the day before. Peyton was never going to believe she and Paul were getting married.

Peyton strolled into the office. "That brother of mine," she growled without finishing the sentence. She didn't have to. Jerry Jenkins, also an electrician, was the bane of his sister's existence. Martina was starting to think he intentionally did things to get under Peyton's skin.

"What has little brother done this time?"

Peyton sat behind the old oak desk, and Martina plopped down in one of the guest chairs across from her.

"I gave him a simple job of wiring a sound system for a new boutique in Mariemont and he screwed it up."

Martina listened as Peyton went on and on about how he had installed the wrong size speakers even though the customer ended up liking them better than what was originally proposed. It was Jerry's turn to take Peyton's wrath. She'd been dealing with something personal for months and instead of talking about whatever was bothering her, she'd been biting everyone's head off.

"Do you want to talk about what's going on?" Martina asked. "Because it sounds like the customer is satisfied. Isn't that what's most important?"

Peyton dropped back in her seat and folded her arms.

"That's very important, but it's also important that Jerry starts doing what he's told to do. What if she hadn't liked the speakers he installed? It would have made us look incompetent."

"What's going on, PJ? We used to be able to talk about anything, but lately, you're pulling further away from all of us."

Peyton sat there staring, but eventually relaxed her shoulders and sighed.

"I think pregnancy is mellowing you out, and I'm not sure how I feel about that." A smile played on her lips. "Any other time you would have told me to get my head out of my butt and quit trippin'."

"No. I would have said you either tell me what's wrong with you or I'm going to beat it out of you!"

They laughed. Martina realized how much she missed hanging out with Peyton. All of the girls tried to get together monthly for a girl's night out, but lately, everyone had been hanging out with their "*boos*" as Christina referred to their significant others. That is, all but Peyton. Since her divorce three years ago, she hadn't dated much and didn't seem to be interested in starting.

Martina and Peyton were closer than the others,

and usually got together weekly, but since Paul came back into Martina's life, that wasn't happening. Not because Martina hadn't tried, but Peyton kept finding excuses for why she couldn't go out or was too busy to get together.

"I don't know what's going on, MJ." Peyton put her elbows on her desk and ran her fingers through her straightened hair. "Seems like I've been saying that a lot lately. I just can't pinpoint exactly, what my problem is."

"Is it work? Are you sick?" Martina threw out a few questions in hopes of getting Peyton to open up. "Is it Dylan?"

Peyton's ex-husband had done a number on her. Not only had he cheated, but he'd also used her to help get him through grad school. Once he graduated, Dylan conveniently decided he no longer loved Peyton. Unfortunately, it took her cousin a while to let go and occasionally, she brought him up in conversation.

"I saw him."

"Who?"

"Dylan. I was at the mall a few months ago and saw him with the woman he was having an affair with." She sighed and rocked back and forth in her office chair. "They were at a jewelry store."

"And you're just mentioning this now?" Martina threw up her hands. "Why didn't you tell me sooner? Never mind that. Are you still pining for him? Do you miss him?"

Peyton shook her head. "No. But what I do miss is the companionship. He wasn't home a lot, especially while working and attending grad school, but he was there enough for me to miss having someone to come home to. And I guess it's been a little hard lately with all of you finding love and having babies…" Her voice trailed off and Martina knew at that moment asking her to stand up for her when she got married might not be the best idea.

"PJ, you're still young. I know you're going to have the family you've always wanted."

She let out a humorless laugh. "Yeah, right. I'll be thirty-five in a couple of months. I've pretty much given up on that idea."

"That's crazy. If love and a *hot* hunk can find me and break down my walls, I have no doubt the same will happen for you."

"Maybe. So what brings you to the office in the middle of the day?" Peyton asked. She logged into the computer on her desk and typed.

"I…" When Martina didn't continue, Peyton looked up.

"What?"

"Well, I came here to ask you something. Now I'm not sure if it's a good idea."

Martina wasn't sure what Peyton saw on her face, but whatever it was had her shaking her head.

"MJ, I think you've met your quota for surprises this month. I'm not sure if I can take another from you … or from anyone else for that matter." She chuckled but stopped when Martina didn't say anything.

"Okay. So this must be serious." Martina remained quiet. She didn't want to put Peyton into a deeper funk, but she also didn't think she could marry Paul without having her there. Sure she could ask one of her other cousins, but PJ was her best friend.

Peyton stood and walked around to the front of

the desk and leaned against it.

"Like you said earlier, you know you can talk to me about anything."

Martina hesitated, but then held out her hand, wiggling her fingers. "Paul asked me to marry him, and I said yes."

Peyton's eyes went wide, and her mouth formed a perfect circle. "Get the heck out of here! Are you serious?"

"Yeah, I know. I can hardly believe it myself."

"First a baby and now marriage? And you said, yes? Miracles never cease! I'm so happy for you. Paul is such a nice guy." Peyton opened her arms, and they hugged. "I guess we have a wedding to plan."

"Well, here's the thing."

"Oh boy. Why do I have a feeling I'm not going to approve of whatever you're about to say?"

"You don't have to approve. You just have to be at Paul's house next Saturday morning, prepared to sign on a dotted line."

Peyton narrowed her eyes, her hands on her hips. "What are you talking about?"

"We're getting married by a judge at Paul's house and have decided that we only want two witnesses. You and Davion."

"What? Grandma is going to have a fit! Are you sure you don't want to have a wedding? You know how disappointed she was when Jada eloped."

"That's because all Jada talked about since she was five was getting married and having a ridiculously big wedding. They don't expect that from me."

Peyton twisted her lips as if thinking. "Okay good point, but—"

"No buts. CJ and Luke are getting married in a

couple of months. So there will be a wedding for everyone to attend."

"Yeah, but everyone probably won't be able to go to Jamaica for her wedding."

Peyton walked back around her desk and grabbed a calendar.

"True." Martina shrugged. "But that's not my problem."

"Maybe not, but don't you want at least some of the family to attend? This is an exciting time for you and Paul. Even if you don't want to do a large wedding, why not have a reception? We can invite the family, and we can even keep it casual. What do you think? Give the family a chance to celebrate with you guys."

"I don't know." Martina rubbed the back of her neck, already feeling anxious that the plans for a reception could get out of hand. She lived a simple, comfortable life on her own terms and even the slightest changes could wig her out. "Peyton, this might not be a good idea. I have finals coming up and—"

"The girls and I will plan the reception. You won't have to do anything."

"Yeah, famous last words."

"Trust me. You can get married by a judge the way you want, and we'll take care of the arrangements for the reception."

Martina left Peyton's office still having doubts about a reception. She trusted her cousin's judgment and knew this plan would please her mother and grandmother. She just hoped the arrangements didn't get out of hand.

*

Martina sighed as she put an extra strip of packing tape on an empty box and tossed the box to the side. Two days before she planned to marry Paul, and she and her cousins were packing up her house.

What was I thinking?

Paul had insisted on getting movers to pack up her things, but she nixed the idea. She already felt as if she was losing control of her whole life. No way was she letting strangers pack her belongings, tossing items all over the place.

She glanced up when Christina started unloading a cabinet and putting the items in three different boxes.

"CJ, why are you separating the glasses from the cups? Everything in that cabinet goes in the same box."

"MJ, your packing system is dumb, and I'm getting a little sick of you yelling at me about everything! If you keep this up, you're going to be doing the rest of this yourself."

"She's right, MJ," Peyton said, pulling pots from a lower cabinet and setting them on the counter. "What's your problem?"

Frustration roared inside of Martina. "You guys are my problem! Why'd you volunteer to help, if you weren't going to pack things the way I want?" Anxiousness and irritability were her constant companions for the last few days, as the moving day and wedding got closer.

"We volunteered so you wouldn't do all of this yourself. You should've let Paul hire the movers like he suggested."

"*You* shouldn't be saying anything to me right now." Martina pointed at Peyton. "It's because of you I'm all stressed out!"

"What?"

"I let you talk me into having a reception, but I can't believe you convinced me to have a big wedding too! I should have just stuck with my original plan." But no, she had let Peyton talk her into moving the wedding date back a week, inviting her mother, their grandparents, the girls, and their spouses to the ceremony. Not to mention, Paul's parents and his sisters. Martina appreciated the extra week, but what started as five people had quickly turned into twenty-five guest at the wedding.

"Martina, it's not like you've had to do much," Peyton said. "We've taken care of everything. You're having a *small* intimate wedding with only a few of us and then everyone else will attend the reception Saturday night. All you have to do is show up."

Martina grabbed a plate, wrapped it in packing paper, and placed it inside one of the boxes that she had just built. She did the same with the next plate, still ignoring Peyton's comment. Martina didn't want a wedding per se, although she liked the idea of her mother and grandparents attending the ceremony. As for a reception, all of the Jenkins clan would attend, making her the center of attention, which she wasn't looking forward to. She talked a big game but didn't like being on display.

"Okay, MJ, I just got off the phone with the dress shop," Jada said from the living room. "We need to get there by two for one last fitting. I'm pretty sure the dress is fine, but we need to be positive that it fits. Hurry and finish whatever you're doing. I need to make a stop before we head that way. Oh and…"

Martina tuned out. There were too many changes going on in her life at the same time.

What was I thinking agreeing to all of this?

Toni strolled into the kitchen carrying a picture box, followed by little Craig, who dragged one of his toys into the living room.

"Did you say you wanted the first guest bedroom to stay as is for staging when the realtor shows the house or was it the second bedroom?"

Martina gripped the next plate with both hands and gritted her teeth, trying to maintain what little control she had left.

"TJ, how many times do I have to tell you? The first one stays as is and everything goes except the bed in the second bedroom. Dang! What is it with all of you?"

Toni dropped the box, and her hands flew to her hips. "I don't know what your problem is, but you need to chill with all of the yelling."

"I'm not yelling!" Martina screamed, slamming the plate on the floor, pieces of ceramic flying everywhere. "Just stop it, dammit! I can't handle any more questions!"

Little Craig started crying, running from the living room to Toni. Everyone spoke at once, and Martina felt like throwing something else.

She closed her eyes tight and gripped the sides of her head, willing herself not to scream again or burst into tears. Her heart pounded wildly, and her hands shook uncontrollably as frustration mixed with a bit of anger battled within her.

I should never have agreed to this. Any of this.

A baby. Moving. Marriage. Martina grasped her head tighter trying to get a grip on her nerves and slow her racing heart, but she was losing the battle. She knew too much stress wasn't good for the baby, but she couldn't seem to get herself together.

"I can't do this. I can't do this. I just can't do this!" she chanted.

Martina didn't know how long she repeated those words before realizing the room had gone quiet.

She slowly opened her eyes and lowered her arms, her breathing still not back to normal.

"You can't do what, Martina?"

Her head jerked up to find Paul standing near the front door and her heart crashed against her chest. Tears pricked the back of her eyes as she met his gaze. She had no idea how much he had witnessed or what else he had heard, but it was clear he'd heard enough.

"Would you ladies excuse us?" he said, as he moved closer to the kitchen area without taking his gaze from her.

"She's pregnant, hormonal and a little crazy. Good luck," Toni said, squeezing Paul's arm as she passed him with little Craig on her hip. "We'll come back in about an hour."

CJ rubbed Martina's back as she, Peyton and Jada headed for the front door, closing it behind them.

Martina was unable to move. Paul's stare had her rooted in place. This was his fault. How had she let him talk her into this...this craziness?

Without saying a word, he removed the broom from the small pantry closet. He grabbed her hand, giving it a slight tug and guided her around the breakfast bar and out of the kitchen. He didn't speak until he released her hand.

"What's going on?" He started sweeping up the pieces of the broken plate.

Martina felt like such an idiot for slamming the

dish to the floor while everyone was so close by. She hadn't been thinking. As a matter of fact, it seemed she hadn't thought for herself in a while.

"Martina," Paul prompted as he kept sweeping. "What's wrong? Talk to me."

"Why didn't you tell me the state had passed the bill regarding the unions?"

For the past few weeks, with final exams, wedding planning, working and a host of other responsibilities, she'd been distracted. It wasn't until earlier that day while watching the news did she find out the bill had passed.

"It was a done deal. There was nothing else to discuss."

"You could have done more to stop it, Paul! I'm starting to think the discussion we had at the cafe was just to pacify me!" she yelled.

"Martina, I was genuinely interested in what you had to say, but you need to understand, I am one man. There were so many more variables involved in that bill," he said calmly, making her angrier. His calmness was one trait she liked about him, but right now, she found it irritating.

"Whatever! Now the government can do whatever the heck they want - or not - when it comes to pay raises, employee evaluations..." She waved her arms around frustrated that she couldn't get her thoughts together and pissed that Paul was now looking at her as if she had lost her mind.

Martina diverted her gaze and paced around the living room, knowing that talking to him about the unions was useless.

"I know what you're trying to do Martina. You're trying to start a fight, but I'm not going there with you. Talk to me and tell me what's on your mind. You didn't answer my question earlier. What can't you do anymore?"

Martina stopped moving and turned to him. Her words stalled in her mouth knowing that what she had on her mind would hurt him. Agony crawled through her body. God knows she didn't want to hurt him. He was the only man she had ever allowed herself to love, and she couldn't see herself with anyone else. Yet...

"Everything is happening too fast," she blurted out.

He set the broom aside and approached her. When he reached for her, she unconsciously took a step back. Shock registered on his face.

"I need ... I need to think, and I can't do that when you're close to me ... or touching me."

He shoved his hands into his pockets but didn't speak. She hated when he got like this, all quiet and composed. As if dealing with all of these changes, at the same time, were like the most natural thing in the world.

"Paul, I'm stressed, overwhelmed and out of control." She glanced down at her ballerina slippers before returning her attention to him. "I don't know if I can do this." She fought back the tears that were threatening to fall.

"Do what?" he finally spoke. "Baby, what can't you do?"

"Any of this!" she screamed, her patience shot. "A baby, moving, marriage... I don't think I can go through with moving in with you and...I don't know if I can marry you."

Emotions flashed across Paul's face and his jaws

clenched. He removed his hands from his pocket and ran one over his mouth and down his chin before letting it fall to his side. He maintained his coolness, but there was a definite hardening of his eyes.

"You're the one who picked the wedding date, Martina, and you said you were sure. You said you were ready. And you said you loved me and wanted us to spend the rest of our lives together."

A few tears slipped through, and Martina quickly swiped them away. "I do love you," she choked out. "I love you so much, but I'm scared to death. I don't know if I can go through with this marriage idea."

She had always been in control of her life, doing what she wanted to and when she wanted to. Lately, all of her control and independence was slipping away, leaving her vulnerable. Vulnerable to heartbreak. She couldn't let that happen. She couldn't lose what little control she had over her life. Yes, she had to think about the baby, but she knew whether they were married or not, Paul would be there for their child.

He shook his head and sighed. She followed his moves as he closed his eyes and ran his hand over his head and down the back of his neck. She had no idea what he was thinking, or where they went from there.

"I love you so much." His words were thick with emotion, and Martina felt as if her heart had split in two. "You and our baby mean the world to me, but I can't force you to be my wife. I know you love me too, and I understand that you're scared. All I can do is tell you that if you give me a chance, give us a chance, I promise you won't regret it. So think about that."

He turned and walked away, but stopped when he

got to the door, his hand on the doorknob.

"I'll be at your grandparents' house, prepared to marry you in two days as planned. You're either going to be there … or you're not. It's your choice."

CHAPTER TWENTY-TWO

"You look like hell," Davion said when he strolled into Steven Jenkins' study, where Paul was camped out.

"I feel like hell."

Paul moved slowly around the room that had been transformed to resemble a small chapel. A floral wedding arch, positioned near an oversized window, stood before twenty-five to thirty cushioned folding chairs that were set up like pews. Bouquets of white, long stem roses in clear vases were mounted on ornamental pedestals, strategically placed around the room. Martina insisted she wanted the wedding small, simple, and intimate. The space was perfect.

Paul stopped at the window that overlooked a massive side yard, gazing out at the snow that fell the night before. He hadn't slept in two days, and it was his fault. Maybe he could have handled Martina's meltdown differently. He should have stayed there and talked the problem out with her, somehow convince her that they were both ready to move forward together.

"She's still not here, just in case you were wondering." Davion stood next to him as they gazed out the window.

Paul said nothing. He and Martina were to be married in two hours and all he could do was wait. He arrived early because he was going crazy at home. He hadn't talked to her since he had left her house, knowing the next move had to be hers.

Paul braced his hands on the window casing and leaned in, exhaustion getting the best of him. He had hoped Martina would be at her grandparents' house waiting for him, but no such luck. The woman was so damn unpredictable until he honestly didn't know if she would show. She didn't think she was ready for marriage. Still he hoped. He hoped she remembered how good they were together. He hoped she would recall the numerous plans they made for the future. More than anything, he hoped she remembered how much he loved her and their unborn child.

"Oh yeah, I forgot to tell you. Myra said that she, your parents, and Janice are on their way."

Paul and his mother had finally made peace. He was glad that she had reached out to him before he had a chance to tell her about the baby and his plans to marry Martina. Otherwise, he wouldn't have known if her sudden change of heart in supporting his plans had to do with the fact that she'd have another grandchild to dote on.

"I had no idea the Jenkins family was rolling in dough like this," Davion said, breaking into Paul's thoughts. "Did you know they have a ballroom in this joint? That's where the reception will be tonight, assuming there's a wedding."

Paul turned to Davion. His first thought was to wrap his hands around his cousin's neck and squeeze, but he was sure that wouldn't make him feel better. And taking his frustrations out on him wouldn't accomplish anything.

All Paul wanted right now was for his baby to walk through those doors, and into his arms.

A knock sounded on the door, and his heart leaped until the door swung open. Craig, Luke, and Zack walked in. The expressions on their faces weren't encouraging, and Paul assumed they didn't have any news on whether Martina had arrived.

Feeling like a deflated balloon, he dropped down in one of the guest chairs.

"I was going to ask how you're holding up, but I guess that's a stupid question." Craig squeezed Paul's shoulder and sat next to him. Zack and Luke turned chairs around until they were all in somewhat of a circle.

"I'm going to let you guys talk. I'll be in the kitchen seeing if they need a taste tester," Davion said on his way out the door.

"If it makes you feel any better, we've all been where you're at, sort of," Zack said. "Jada put me through hell before we got married, but being with her is worth every single gray hair on my head."

"And I'm sure you've heard all about what I went through trying to convince Toni to marry me. Let's just say I know your pain, and I wouldn't wish it on anyone. But that woman is truly a gift from God. I would go through the mayhem again if it meant keeping her in my life," Craig added.

They all turned their gazes to Luke, who sat back in his seat and crossed his arms. "I'll never forget the day Zack told me he and Craig had formed a support group for men who date a Jenkins' girl."

On that, Paul laughed, and everyone else joined in. "I wish someone would have told me about this group months ago."

"I know right? But I have to tell you, Paul. CJ and the Jenkins family are the best things that have ever happened to me," Luke continued. "But dating her has been wild and crazy as hell at times. I never know what to expect. Just when I think I have her figured out, she flips a switch and shows me a different side of her. Every day I have fallen more and more in love with her."

Listening to the guys share stories about their adventures with the Jenkins women let Paul know that they indeed did understand what he'd been through dating Martina. She was like no other woman he had ever known. Her fire and huge personality kept his boring world interesting, and she was the one he wanted to grow old with.

"Ahh, I see I'm right on time," Steven Jenkins walked into the room. Martina's grandfather was a big man. Tall and fit for his age, he had a presence about him that would make anyone stand at attention.

They all stood, but he waved them off.

"Relax. I figured I'd come and let you know that my granddaughters have arrived." He sat next to Luke. "All of them." He looked at Paul pointedly.

Paul probably would have crashed to the floor with relief had he not been sitting down. But he still wasn't going to let himself get too comfortable until he actually heard Martina say, "I do."

*

Martina sat at the antique makeup table as Jada

touched up her makeup for the second time. The last couple of days had been the worse days of Martina's life, and though she didn't think she had any tears left, she felt them swell in her eyes.

Jada sighed. "You know I'm not the most patient person in the world, and you're trying my patience today with all of these tears. What the heck? Did you save them up for the last thirty-one years just for today?"

Martina laughed. Never had she cried so much. Not even when she was ten and her dog, Tipsy, got ran over by a car.

"I didn't want any makeup in the first place. You're the one who's insisting I wear some."

"You can't get married without makeup." Jada went back to work adding blush to her cheeks.

Martina thought about Paul waiting downstairs. Shame spun inside of her, and she felt awful for the way she behaved the other day. Toni insisted her actions were probably caused by fear, exhaustion, and pregnancy hormones. Martina didn't know much about hormones, but she could admit that she was nervous. She was scared about becoming and being a wife. If she let Paul walk out of her life, it would be the biggest mistake she ever made.

Her eyes filled with tears and she absently swiped them away with the back of her hand.

Jada cursed. "MJ! You just messed up the work I did on your eyes. She tossed the makeup compact onto the bed and plopped down in the chair near the window. "I quit."

"Are we almost ready in here?" Carolyn asked when she waltzed into the room wearing a short, champagne colored dress that stopped just above her knees with matching shoes. They had decided the wedding colors would be champagne, black, and white. Martina couldn't ever remember seeing her mother look so beautiful.

"I'm ready, but MJ keeps crying, messing up her makeup. I'm not doing it again." Jada crossed her arms and leg, her foot swinging back and forth bringing attention to her red-bottom shoe.

"Well, I can't help it," Martina sobbed.

"Oh, sweetheart." Carolyn sat on the bench next to her and reached for Martina's hand. "It's okay to be a little nervous, but you being here means you've chosen love over fear. Now all you have to do is believe that you and Paul are going to make it. I have no doubt you two are going to have a wonderful marriage."

"Yeah, if she ever lets us finish getting her ready," Jada added.

Carolyn laughed and kissed her daughter on the cheek. "Be nice and let Jada fini—"

"I'm tired of her, Auntie," Jada mumbled and snatched the makeup compact off the bed. "I'm just wasting my time."

Carolyn gave Jada a one-arm hug and kissed her cheek. "Thanks, sweetie. I'm going to leave you girls alone. I'm going downstairs to check on the preparations for the reception."

A minute after Carolyn left, Peyton, Christina, and Toni rushed through the door.

"Okay, everything is all set for the ceremony. Let's go," Peyton said.

Martina wrung her hands. Biting her lower lip, she made eye contact with Peyton.

"What?" Peyton asked and stood in front Martina.

"Don't tell me you—"

"Hold up." Toni stood next to Peyton. "I stayed up with you all last night, listening to you go on and on about how much you love Paul and can't live without him," Toni seethed. "You're going down those stairs if I have to drag you kicking and screaming!"

"Would you just chill, Toni?" Martina said.

"Well, what's with the look?" Peyton asked.

"I want you guys to go and get Paul. I need to talk to him."

"We can't get him! It's bad luck to see the bride before the wedding," Christina said.

"Just go and get him." Martina stood, still wringing her hands.

Toni threw up her arms. "Let's just go and get him. He's the calm to her crazy. Let him deal with her," Toni grumbled as she hurried to the door, the rest of them right behind her.

Seconds later, Paul appeared in the doorway looking like the cover model for GQ magazine.

Martina's heart pounded double time while he approached with the confidence of a man who knew what he wanted and wasn't afraid to take it. A flare of excitement soared through her body as he took in the simple, white dress that stopped just above her knees. Martina couldn't remember the designer's name, but she had fallen in love with the garment the moment Jada made her try it on.

"You look absolutely stunning." Paul's soothing voice wrapped around her like a soft blanket.

Martina swallowed hard to free the lump in her throat. He smelled as good as he looked and desire stirred within her.

"Thank you."

"Since you're here, I assume you've decided to do me the honor of being my wife."

Not trusting her voice, Martina nodded.

"I'm glad." He cupped her face and caressed her cheeks.

"I'm so sorry for the way I behaved and what I said to you the other day. I had a temporary moment of insanity, but I'm ready."

Paul grinned. "I understand. I'm just glad you came around. So this is what we're going to do. We're going downstairs. We are going to profess our love to each other in front of our family. When that's done, we're going to eat and dance at our reception, but we won't stay long."

"No?"

"No, because I'm taking you on a smoking-hot honeymoon where we're going to eat, play and make love all…night…long under the moonlight. Would that work for you?"

A smile tugged at the corner of Martina's mouth and for the first time in days. She knew marrying Paul was going to be the best decision of her life.

"Yes that works, but if you want, we can just skip the reception and go straight to the part about making love all night long."

Paul laughed. "Yeah, I guess that's an option, but after what your cousins have been through in setting all of this into motion, I don't think we'd get out of here alive."

"Good point. They did threaten my life a few times these last couple of days. Let's go get married."

"Okay, but first there's something I have wanted to do since I walked into the room."

He lowered his head and the moment his lips touched hers, Martina knew they were going to have an awesome life together.

EPILOGUE

Two Months Later

"Are you sure your eyes are closed?" Martina asked Paul as she navigated the truck through the streets of downtown Cincinnati.

"Yes, but it doesn't matter. Even if they were open, I wouldn't be able to see anything with this tight scarf over my eyes."

Martina laughed and pulled into the gravel parking lot, dodging potholes along the way.

"Okay, don't move. I'm coming around to help you out of the truck.

"Martina, are you sure that's a good idea? I can—"

"Paul, I'm fine."

He'd been overprotective since their scare, three weeks ago when she'd had some spotting and rushed to the emergency room. That was probably the only time Martina had ever seen him shaken up. Normally he was a pillar of strength and calm. That day, they both had been a nervous wreck until they found out that she and the baby were fine.

Since then, Paul had been watching her like a hawk, not wanting her to do anything or go anywhere alone. When he mentioned her taking a leave from work, Martina had to set him straight. She would go crazy and drive everyone around her nutty, especially him, if she couldn't work. After a bit of hesitation, he agreed.

Holding Paul's hand, Martina guided him across the parking lot and didn't stop until she had him standing in front of a building. A week earlier he had completed his six-year term as a U.S. Senator and seemed to be at peace with not being in politics anymore. But Martina knew that if she didn't find something to help occupy his time, he would drive her batty.

"Okay, you can remove the blindfold."

He yanked it off and blinked several times before zoning in on the building.

"Oookay." He turned to her and shrugged.

"This is your new restaurant."

His brows shot up. "What?" He turned back to the old building that had once been an Italian restaurant and rushed up to it. Holding his hand over his eyes like a visor, he peeked through one of the windows that wasn't boarded up. "You bought me a restaurant?"

"Heck no! I don't have that type of money," Martina chuckled. Technically she did have access to those types of funds according to Paul. Though she was willing, he didn't want her to sign a prenup, explaining that whatever he had was hers.

"I thought this building would be perfect for *you* to buy. The size is exactly what you wanted. We can tweak the layout easily, and the location is perfect. Want to see inside?"

Again his brows shot up in surprise. "You have a key?"

She dangled the keys in front of him. "Apparently your name carries a lot of weight. Shall we?"

"Definitely. It's too cold for you and our little girl to be outside."

Martina smiled as he unlocked the door. The day before, they had found out the sex of the baby. Though she didn't care about their child's gender, Paul had wanted a girl. She was shocked that he hadn't wanted a boy, but apparently he was a glutton for punishment when it came to having another Jenkins' girl in the family.

Martina walked beside him, explaining what she knew about the building and its previous use. She also pointed out repair needs as they strolled through the entire facility. She couldn't wait to tackle some of the projects if he decided to purchase the place. At five months pregnant, she was getting to the stage where some of her work had to be delegated to others, but she had no problem bossing people around.

"So what do you think?" Martina asked.

Paul stood in the center of what would be the main dining area and glanced around again before training his attention on her.

He pulled her close. "I think you are the most fascinating woman I've ever known, and I give thanks every day to God for bringing you back into my life."

"Thank you, but I was talking about the building. What do you think of the building?"

He grinned. "Oh. The building is nice too."

She shoved against his chest. "I mean can you see

opening a restaurant here? Could this be the place?"

He nodded, gazing around again. "It has potential and with the ideas you tossed out, I think it could definitely work."

"Awesome! I'll hook you up with the realtor, and we can go from there."

"Sounds good." He reached for her hand and turned serious. "Thank you for doing this, for believing and supporting my dream. It means a lot to me."

Martina wrapped her arms around his waist and gazed into his eyes. "You mean a lot to me. I never thought I could be as happy as I've been since you came back into my life *and* we're having a baby. Never in a million years did I see my life going in this direction. I'm so glad you didn't give up on me."

"I love you too much." Paul cupped her cheek in the palm of his hand. "I'll never give up on you. I'll never give up on us."

"Me either. I love you."

The End

If you enjoyed this book by
Sharon C. Cooper, consider leaving
a review on any online book site,
review site, or social media outlet.

ABOUT THE AUTHOR

Award-winning and bestselling author, Sharon C. Cooper, spent 10 years as a sheet metal worker. And while enjoying that unique line of work, she attended college in the evening and obtained her B.A. in Business Management with an emphasis in Communication. Sharon is a romance-a-holic - loving anything that involves romance with a happily-ever-after, whether in books, movies or real life. She writes contemporary romance, as well as romantic suspense and enjoys rainy days, carpet picnics, and peanut butter and jelly sandwiches. When Sharon is not writing or working, she's hanging out with her amazing husband, doing volunteer work or reading a good book (a romance of course). To read more about Sharon and join her email mailing list, visit www.sharoncooper.net.

Other Titles by Sharon C. Cooper:

Jenkins Family Series (Contemporary Romance)
Best Woman for the Job (Short Story Prequel)
Still the Best Woman for the Job (book 1)
All You'll Ever Need (book 2)
Tempting the Artist (book 3)
Negotiating for Love – (book 4)
Seducing the Boss Lady – (book 5) – *Coming Soon*

Reunited Series (Romantic Suspense)
Blue Roses (book 1)
Secret Rendezvous (Prequel)
Rendezvous with Danger (book 2)
Truth or Consequences (book 3)
Operation Midnight (book 4)

Stand Alones
Something New ("Edgy" Sweet Romance)
Legal Seduction (Harlequin Kimani)
Sin City Temptation (Harlequin Kimani)
A Dose of Passion (Harlequin Kimani)
Model Attraction (Harlequin) – *Coming April 2016*